"Shocking and ███ ████ █████ ████ gruesome, desp███ ██ ████ ████ protect those we ██████ ███ ███ ████ ███ ████ █████ the death, and taste the terror on every page."
— **Tim Lebbon**
New York Times bestselling author of *The Silence & The Last Storm*

"A chilling tale for the end of the world."
— **Priya Sharma**
British Fantasy & Shirley Jackson Award winning author of *Ormeshadow*

"If ecological, apocalyptic, survival horror is a thing, then O'Connor has tapped the vein of those genres and bled them dry. A gripping and tension-filled read."
— **Ross Jeffery**
Bram Stoker Award-nominated author of *Tome*

"With echoes of Cormac McCarthy's *The Road* and John W. Campbell Jr.'s *Who Goes There?*, *The Swarm* is a tension-filled apocalyptic nightmare... as stark and unrelenting and chilling as its Arctic setting."
— **Richard Chizmar**
New York Times best-selling author

BY SEAN O'CONNOR

THE
SWARM

BY SEÁN O'CONNOR

The Mongrel

Weeping Season

The Blackening

Keening Country

Revelations
Horror Writers for Climate Action

The Swarm

THE
SWARM

SEÁN O'CONNOR

IDOLUM

Idolum Publishing
Dublin, Ireland

Legal Deposit and Library Cataloguing in Publication Data.
A catalogue record for this book is available from The National
Library of Ireland.

Typeset in 11pt Bookman Old Style
Interior Design by Kenneth W. Cain

ISBN: 978-1-8383788-9-9

1 3 5 7 9 10 8 6 4 2

First Edition

For Samuel

Never Change

"Vast and awful, the night hardens between us."

— 40 Watt Sun

PART ONE
REMNANTS

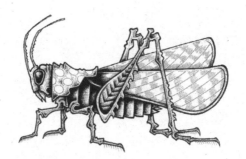

Jeremy Boucher reached out to calm his son, Rémy, as he whimpered in his sleep. Another bad dream. They were becoming all too regular – especially during the dead of night when the fuselage interior was at its coldest. He pulled the boy in closer, hoping his body heat would help sooth him back to sleep, stroking his forehead as he sang in a soft whisper to him, wishing for first light to come. Loud noises in this place of absolute solitude could bring a death sentence, and the reavers didn't care what they ate, as long as it was alive.

The dawning light inched in on the back of a ferocious Arctic wind. He left the boy sleeping, wrapped up well, and went outside. Though he couldn't be sure, he figured they'd already entered winter – he'd lost track of the calendar quite a while ago. He shielded his face as he looked in every direction, seeing white nothingness to the horizon. Their crashed plane, now a makeshift camp, had survived another long night.

A few feet from the Basler's cargo door, two boreholes in the ice overflowed with water. He sat on his hunkers and pulled up the fishing lines. Nothing from the sea this morning. Thoughts of another day without breakfast worried him. He replaced the bait with something shiny and went to wake the boy.

Inside the plane, he lit a gas-powered stove, which soon turned clumps of snow into warm water. Something in the distance caught his attention, possibly a bird singing but he couldn't be sure. He doubted it in such extreme conditions.

Rémy shivered while cupping his

bowl, listening to his father say grace, then complained of hunger.

Boucher didn't reply – nothing he could say would take the pain away. Instead, he hoped some warm liquid would take the cold out of his thinning body. He assisted the boy getting dressed.

Routine was important to Boucher. It kept him from going insane in a bleak world of insignificance. At first, Rémy was interested in their daily tasks but when days turned to weeks and weeks to months, the sheer mundanity had him turning inward out of sheer boredom.

Winter had arrived, that much he was sure of. The nights were longer, the water had iced over, and, after the low sun set on pale daylight, the bitter cold of the Arctic Circle became consistent.

Most mornings, he'd teach Rémy what he could about survival. Simple things, like tying knots properly, and because the boy showed an interest, he would give him a tour of the Basler's cockpit. Learning to operate a crashed plane seemed useless but it fuelled the boy's imagination and allowed him to dream about flying away someday. He was only allowed to play with his figurines and read books before bedtime.

At lunchtime, they inspected the boreholes but found nothing again. Disappointed, the boy wanted to return to the plane to play with his toys, but Boucher pulled rank and reminded him of the importance of their routine, which, in turn, signalled their first argument of the day, with the boy venting his frustration: "We never catch anything anymore."

"We have to keep the faith, son."

"Why?"

"Help will come soon."

"When?"

"When our signal is picked up."

"From the beacon?"

"Yes. From the beacon."

When the sun was at its highest, though still weak, the wind eased off, allowing them to head east towards the white hills. While they weren't far, the trek to the summit was hardest on days with empty stomachs.

4

From the viewpoint, Boucher surveyed the landscape, keeping his desperation hidden, adding any new features he spotted to his hand-drawn map. He felt sure a fjord lay somewhere close by – the last thing he'd seen before their plane came down. But from high ground, it always seemed to be lost in the vast Arctic waste.

A few hundred feet from the foot of the hill, what remained of their plane reflected in the sun. Beyond it, nothing but endless white. Behind him, the hill turned sharp and jagged –too advanced for the boy to trek in his weak state. He needed nourishment but it wasn't coming to them, and the thought of starving to death during an Arctic winter terrified him, especially if he died before Rémy.

Hours later, at the highest point they could reach, Boucher charged a dynamo in a handmade rescue beacon – patched together from the plane's transmitter.

The boy hated this part of the day, mostly because he had to watch hope build in his father's eyes when the beacon started blinking, then die hours later when their signal went unanswered. "I want to go back to our plane."

"One more hour, Rémy."

"Why?"

"Someone might catch the signal this time."

"And then what?"

"We might get away from here."

"Where?"

"South. Hopefully…"

"Is it warm there?"

"Warmer than here."

"But you said home was gone."

"Come here and help me."

"No."

Normally, his father would correct him when he got sassy. However, not this time. Instead, he nodded once and squeezed his shoulder. Though the cold was numbing, his father's touch felt good. So much had happened to them, with those reavers taking their world away, along with… his mother. He wouldn't have blamed his father for lashing out but it felt pretty good that he didn't – something of a victory – he'd been listened to. They continued to charge the dynamo, hoping for the beacon to be heard.

An hour later, they trekked down the hill in silence, heading for their plane. Hungry and cold, he could barely feel his toes. As they approached the boreholes, panting with the effort, his father stopped him. "You hear that?"

It took a moment for a jingling sound on the breeze to fully register against the backdrop of cold silence. "Yes!" Excitement surged through him as he readied to sprint.

"Don't run."

He turned back, "Why?"

"I told you before, there are crevasses all over this place."

He curled his toes. "Under the snow?"

"Yes. Always take care before stepping. If you fall into one, I might never see you again."

Another lesson – one to remember.

Snow crunched underfoot as they trudged towards the boreholes. The jingling grew louder as they got closer, both almost gasping with exhilaration. One of the lines danced and bounced, the makeshift chime ringing. His dad grabbed the line and it went taut. With a smile, he began pulling it from the icy water. His brows furrowed with the effort but when brown scales revealed themselves, they both could hardly contain themselves.

"Woah, it's a big one," Rémy screamed, almost clapping.

Moments later, the large brown fish was out and flopping in the snow, his father's face etched with pure joy.

"That's the biggest fish I've ever seen, Dad."

His father didn't reply, but a joyous laugh escaped his lips. Then they both went silent, watching the fish flap as it struggled for life. Its mouth gawped, the eyes almost bulging as it gyrated, too far from the borehole to make it back to safety. It didn't take long before it became still, dead in the cold silence.

A strong smell filled the fuselage. Normally, they would eat a catch raw to avoid wasting the lighter fuel and what little gas was left in the portable stove. But this was a special occasion. A fish of this size needed to be cooked and enjoyed. Nothing boosted spirits like a warm meal. The plump fillet sizzled in the pan and their stomachs growled in anticipation.

"Can we eat it all?" the boy said.

"No."

"Why?"

"We need to keep some for breakfast... and bait."

"Okay."

"It's a cod," Boucher said.

"What?"

"The fish. It's a cod. Big one, too. Hopefully we can use it to catch more like it."

"Fish eat fish?"

"Some do. I guess."

"Do people eat people?"

"I hope not..."

Silence returned as they devoured their first proper meal in weeks. Outside, the sunlight faded and a dull grey dusk cloaked the landscape. Boucher placed the remains of the fish outside beneath a layer of snow. Afterwards, the interior was prepared for night-time mode by covering the windows and locking the door, then they fell asleep with satisfied stomachs.

Boucher woke with a fright. He grabbed about, searching for the boy's sleeping bag, but failed to touch anything. When he sat up, it surprised him to see light inside the fuselage. Disoriented, he scrambled to his feet and searched the plane. He'd told the boy, if he needed to use the toilet, the rule was that he had to wake him. Now the kid was nowhere to be found.

Outside, bloodstains in the snow by the entrance struck fear into his heart. Panicked, he scanned the wilderness and, to his delight, the boy was standing by one of the boreholes.

"Rémy! What are you doing?"

"Dad, the fish. They're all gone."

Snow crunched under angry footsteps as Boucher ran towards him. He grabbed the boy's shoulders, squeezed as he shook him. "Don't ever scare me like that again."

"I'm okay. I'm okay!"

He released his grip and hugged him. "You have to tell me if you're going outside. It's not safe."

"But the sun is up. Reavers can't get us when the sun is up." He looked up, his eyes full of innocence.

He was right, of course. It took Boucher a few minutes to calm himself and regain focus. The fishing lines had been pulled from the water and abandoned. He studied the scene and noticed markings in the snow. Animal prints – he was sure of it. Large ones, too. The tracks led to the plane.

"Get back inside now," he ordered.

"Why?"

"Don't argue with me. Get inside, now!"

He slammed the Basler's door shut. The boy sat on his bedding, his eyes wide as Boucher paced from side to side, looking through the round windows, searching.

"Where are you?" he repeated to himself.

"What is it, Dad?"

11

He looked at the boy, then resumed patrolling, "Bear. I think. It must have been drawn by the smell of last night's dinner."

"Why?"

"Cause he's probably just as hungry as we are."

"Because of the reavers?"

"Probably."

"But they only come at night, right?"

"Yes. Which means the bear came at first light and could still be around here somewhere."

About an hour later, Boucher felt it was safe enough for him to leave – the daily tasks had to be done and he reckoned the bear had moved on. Well, he hoped. Then, with no other choice, he lied to the boy, telling him everything was going to be okay. While Rémy was young, he wasn't as naive as he'd initially thought but a little reassurance would do no harm. "I have to go to the beacon."

"Why?"

"You know why, Rémy."

"What if the bear comes back?"

"Then you stay quiet and keep the doors shut."

"But I don't want to be on my own..."

Boucher didn't know what to say. He hugged the boy and slipped outside, taking his time – watching. Nothing but cold silence, with an odd snow flurry falling beneath a canopy of grey cloud. The fresh tracks and bloodstains sent a rush of anxiety through him. No way could he leave the boy here. He turned back and opened the door.

"Right, come on, let's grab our gear and get moving."

"Okay."

They set out along the white top towards the hill, Boucher keeping the boy close – each the other's world. A bitter wind cut right through them as they climbed. When they reached their spot, he used the hand crank to charge the beacon, wishing with all his might for the signal to be heard. He looked to the sky, seeing only cloud, with no sign of life in any direction.

"Dad..."

He looked down and Rémy tapped his lower lip. It took him a moment to realize that his lip was bleeding from being clamped between his teeth.

The wind grew stronger, sharper. Rémy shivered, barely able to keep himself still for more than a few seconds, his teeth chattering as he ducked his head beneath his shoulder in a futile attempt at shelter.

Boucher wanted to stay another hour, but the boy wasn't able so he was left with no choice but to give up. As he packed up his things, Rémy jumped to his feet and pointed towards the bottom of the hill, "Dad, Look!"

"Where?"

"Right there." He pointed to what seemed like a plain white backdrop.

Within the nothingness, a faint movement caught Boucher's eye and he focused in, realizing that it was larger than he'd imagined, with powerful limbs. *That thing would rip us to shreds.*

He pulled the boy down into the snow. "Don't make a sound," he whispered, failing to hide the terror in his voice. The large white beast seemed content enough wandering along, stopping every few steps to sniff the air. They watched for what could have been minutes, or an hour, waiting for the bear to move on out of sight. Thankfully, it hadn't caught their scent.

With all his focus on the foraging animal, he almost missed the beep, not looking back until a second one had his heart in his mouth. He turned to see a small green bulb flashing. The beacon beeped again. And again. And again. Horrified, he scrambled over to the device and pressed buttons on the panel, cursing as he failed to stop the repeating noise. Sweat stung his eyes as panic set in.

"Dad?" the boy called, his voice high.

"I'm trying."

"Dad, the He rose to his feet, his eyes locking with the bear's, staring back at him from the foot of the hill. A stand-off, sound-tracked by the intermittent high-pitched beeping. Both man and beast refused to break the connection, until the unmistakable drone of a plane caught their attention. He searched the sky and his heart wrenched when the aircraft appeared, with black smoke trailing from one of its engines. Then it vanished beyond the hills.

To his relief, the noise spooked the beast, causing it to disappear back into the white haze. Or, at least, that's what he hoped. With a sense of urgency, he gripped the boy's hand and cursed their failed chance of being rescued – their first in months.

"Damn that fucking bear!"

At the foot of the hill, Boucher removed a knife from his pants' pocket and flicked the blade out with a snapping sound. He didn't say anything to the boy, signalling him to watch instead, showing him an engraving on its handle: *To My One & Only, Love, Vicky.*

"Mom?" the boy said.

"A gift from our last anniversary..." He proceeded to run the blade along his palm, grimacing as the steel invaded his flesh. It had to be done. He closed the knife with his good hand and clenched the other into a fist, squeezing until blood oozed through his fingers.

The boy watched with wonder and confusion.

"Come on, Rémy. We have to get back."

When they arrived at their makeshift home, Boucher dressed his wound as the boy watched, his puzzlement obvious in his creased brows, no doubt wanting to ask why he'd left a trail of blood from the hill to the plane.

Boucher looked at him, knowing he was a little overwhelmed. "Keep your spirits up, son."

"Why?"

"Because that plane means others are still out there."

"Can we go home now?"

"Maybe."

"What about the bear? Will he hurt us?"

"No, I won't let it. We're safe in here."

"What if he comes back?"

Boucher nodded to the trail of blood

across the snow. "I want him to."

Eerie silence. They watched from a circular cabin window in the safety of the fuselage. The boy asked repeatedly if the bear would come. Boucher didn't answer. He didn't want to feed his anxiety, focusing instead on the sky, watching it dim as a gathering darkness crept across the land. The days were so short now but they couldn't stay outside once daylight diminished.

The boy studied the trail of blood from the plane to the boreholes, where their leftover cod was stacked neatly in a small mound near the cargo door. "Should we make some noise?" he asked.

"Not yet."

"Why?"

"I want to get a good look at him."

The boy got scared after dark. Usually, they'd spend it huddled in their sleeping bags, fearing the terror that came with the night. Although on this particular one, Boucher couldn't help but admire the clear moonlit sky. Stars twinkled and, somewhere in the distance, a faint green glow danced. Something whisked across the sky – a shooting star? A satellite? He couldn't be sure.

Then there was noise. They both stood straight, sweat glistening on their faces. It happened again, getting closer. Scoffing and snuffling, an unmistakable drone of a large mammal.

"He's here," Boucher whispered.

The beast came into view and made a cautious approach to the fish. Boucher couldn't help but notice its behaviour, acting careful instead of launching a voracious attack like he assumed any hungry predator would. Maybe it wasn't just humanity that had to adjust to the new world. But knowing the dangers of the night well, he waited for the beast to indulge.

With a growl, it snapped up the fish, then sniffed around the boreholes, tapping the surface water with its large paw. Boucher figured it must be starving to risk being out just after dark. Animals learnt that survival trick quicker than people. But this bear was breaking the rules, moonlight illuminating its fur, making it hard to miss.

"On the count of three... make as much noise as you can," he ordered.

"Okay."

"One. Two. Three!"

They jumped up and down, screaming, banging against the inner walls of the wrecked aircraft, punching and kicking, until the bear took an interest in the ruckus.

"It's working, Rémy," he shouted. "Keep it up."

The animal approached, tentative at first, then, as if irritated, it charged, pulling up short when the plane didn't move. It sniffed around, looking for the source of the noise. Then it raised up and pressed its large paws and weight against the plane; the force could be felt all over as the thing rocked from the beast's brute strength.

"Keep shouting!"

The bear roared, as if in retaliation to the taunting, its hungry eyes fixated on them. Boucher backed away from the window and, with his good hand, pulled out a rescue flare and headed towards the tail end of the craft, where he lifted a panel to the outside. The smell of sulphur engulfed the fuselage as he disappeared in a plume of red smoke.

"Dad?" the boy called, his voice shaking.

"Get down, Rémy."

He emerged from the cloud, pulled down the panel, and ran back, checking the windows as he passed. The distraction worked – the bear had gone to investigate. He held the boy close, pulled the blankets over them, and shushed him. "Don't make a sound."

Outside, out of sight, the bear growled – probably a frustrated reaction to the burning flare. Soon the beast went silent, and their focus shifted to a faint hum in the distance.

"Here they come," the boy said, clutching his father tight.

At first, it seemed like a low buzzing, but soon it increased to an intense drone that bore down like a wave and engulfed the plane.

The bear roared, bellowing its defiance, but that soon turned to yelps and screeches of pain. Boucher kept his eyes closed as he followed the action. The plane shook, and he reckoned the beast must have fallen against it, its reactive yells and roars continuing, until the droning enveloped them.

"Can I go see?" the boy asked.

"Shut up!"

"I want to see them, Dad."

"No."

Waves of scraping and tapping, from what Boucher guessed were tiny clawed feet, reverberated around the plane. Clicking and buzzing followed in the absence of any bear sounds. The boy, eyes wide, quivered at the unmistakable squelching of flesh, followed by a final agonizing cry. The bear was dead.

He held Rémy closer, cupping his ears, then closed his eyes and silently prayed for morning light.

An hour after sunrise and they still hadn't emerged from beneath the blankets. Dead silence and Arctic cold filled the plane, along with the lingering smell of the flare from the night before. Clouds of vapour rose from them as warm breath met cool air. They were awake but hadn't spoken a word – it had been one of the longest nights of their lives.

"Are we safe?" the boy eventually asked, his voice raw and croaky.

"I think so."

"Are they gone?"

Boucher told him to wait, then got up and went to investigate. Outside the windows, bloodstains and disturbed snow displayed the bear's fight against the night. The quiet was unsettling, almost unnerving. When he plucked up the courage to open the door, the stench of death and blood attacked his senses. Red snow created a trail to the tail end of the craft.

He ignored the cold and jumped down, red and white snow crunching as he approached – his gaze fixed on the mutilated remains of the large beast. The reavers had stripped it down to the bone

23

in a feeding frenzy, leaving nothing but a hollow frame. Satisfied that his plan worked as intended, he signalled to the boy to come see, then packed up his things and prepared for the daily tasks.

Two days passed and the light diminished. The normality of their routine kept them going and Boucher's hand was healing nicely into a scar he intended to tribute to the bear. At the beacon, he adjusted and added to his map the best he could, then debated with himself if it was time to leave yet – even if he couldn't find the fjord. From somewhere in his memory, he knew there was a research station beside it, and getting to that base would be their best shot at survival. An Arctic winter meant near-permanent darkness for a long period of time – this much he knew – and even in the best of health, they'd never survive it holed up in the wreckage.

"Come here, Rémy. You need to learn how to use this thing."

"Why?"

"Because you need to learn these

things."

"I don't want to," he snapped.

"Listen to your father, Rémy."

"No."

He rested his head in his hands, let out a frustrated sigh, and fought back the urge to argue. After a deep breath, he placed a hand on the boy's shoulder. "If something happens to me, you need to know how to do these things."

The boy stood silent, clearly trying to work it out in his head. One eye glistened but he didn't cry. "I want to stay in our plane."

"We can't stay in the plane forever. It's too dangerous."

"I'm scared."

"I know. Me too, son. But the long night is coming. And with it, those things..."

The boy watched him charge the beacon. After, they sat in silence overlooking the white expanse. Boucher decided it would be best to give the fishing holes a couple more days, determining that south-west would be their best hope for salvation.

They returned to the Basler and began packing for what would be an arduous trip.

"You can't take everything with you," he said.

"Why?"

"We have a long walk ahead. We only have room for essentials."

The boy sat in protest, looking over his belongings. "Why do you always leave everything behind?"

"We have no choice, Rémy."

"That's what you said about Mom."

"We don't have time for this now."

"I'm not leaving," he cried. "You made me leave Mom and now you're making me leave my stuff."

He knelt beside the boy, looked him in the eye, and promised him that everything would be okay – a lie whiter than the snow-covered land surrounding them.

Using at his hand-drawn map, he plotted the best course for them to take. Without a working compass, it was hard to tell exact south-west. While the sun rose from the east and set in the west, the slow change in season disoriented him, and the reality was the goddam fjord could be anywhere.

He told the boy that once they got moving, he'd have to keep up, but his weak body was struggling with the basics already – the poor lad didn't even have the strength to lug a light backpack as far as the boreholes, never mind shoulder it along with the weight of Boucher's pilot uniform. It was big but would help keep the cold off.

After a few alterations, the boy was ready. Boucher took a step back, admiring him for a moment. "Captain Rémy Boucher."

"I don't want to be the captain."

"And I didn't want my plane landing in the middle of nowhere, son. We came so close to hitting the ice, but the snow saved us. And now we have to deal with it or else–"

"Or else what?"

"We'll die." He grimaced at the harshness of his reply.

27

"Good. It's better than walking in the cold."

"Rémy, please. I'm doing the best I can here."

The boy didn't reply. Boucher had insisted on him wrapping up extra-warm for the journey but worried about his ability to trek a long distance. What choice did they have? They couldn't stay here.

They would set out at sunrise, when the coast should be clear. He'd urged the boy to get a good night's sleep but, instead, he spent most of his last night in the plane saying goodbye to his toys.

Morning twilight crept along the horizon. Boucher took it in, forgetting for a while about all the possible problems that lay ahead. The journey south-west, using a made-up map, was the least of his worries. His concern was for the boy, about him being malnourished and underweight, never mind emotionally broken. He was probably marching the lad into certain death. But they couldn't stay at the plane with the winter hardening, with no supplies or realistic prospect of rescue. The sound of their growling stomachs would surely attract reavers.

He helped the boy dress, finding it hard to ignore his whimpering. With an encouraging hug, they took deep breaths and set out across the vast white plains. It didn't take long before fatigue set into his legs. Whatever he felt, the boy would be a hell of a lot worse. Ice hung from his beard, now stiff and frozen, the only relief coming from working his jaw left to right to ease the tightness.

He called behind but got no answer. Then he called again.

Silence.

With a surge of panic, he turned to find him far behind, sitting on the snow with his head in his hands.

"Rémy!" he shouted, but the boy didn't respond. He trudged back, angry with him for stopping without calling out. It was too dangerous out in the open. They had to stay close. When he closed the gap between them, he found the boy sobbing.

"You can't just stop like this, Rémy."

"My legs hurt."

Whatever lecture he was about to unleash vanished as soon as he heard the boy's voice – weak and defeated. His heart sank at the sorry state before him. Instead of giving out, he opted to sit next to him. They huddled together, shivering against the biting cold.

"What was Mom like?"

Taken aback by the question, he took a moment before answering. "Beautiful."

The boy looked to the sky for a long moment. "I don't know what beautiful looks like."

Boucher took a minute to reflect, trying to ignore the cold. "Well... she was a petite woman, with big blue eyes that could melt your heart. Combine that with lovely long brown hair and one hell of an infectious laugh. She was our everything."

"I don't remember."

"Well, she lives on in you and she'd want you to stay with me and be safe."

The vastness around them was awe-inspiring and terrifying. Boucher debated whether to keep heading south-west or return to the plane – a dilemma he needed to resolve before sundown, which came earlier each day. The pale sky rose from the horizon, above the white void. It was mostly clear, with few clouds. He scanned all directions, searching for dark clouds and the next wave of bad weather. Thankfully, there was nothing obvious except some smoke rising in the east.

Smoke?

"What the...? Rémy, look over there."

"No."

"Rémy, look. Is that smoke or am I seeing things?"

The boy glanced in the direction his father was pointing and, for the first time in weeks, a glimmer of hope sparked in his eyes. "Yeah, Dad. I see it, too."

Boucher kicked his heels into the snow. "We'll never make it over there before dark."

The boy didn't reply. No surprise. He had a good idea what was going through the kid's head. Everything that happens in the dead new world was more than likely dangerous, and carried a risk to life.

No doubt, he wished to go back to the plane, which might be their only option right now.

He got up, assessing the findings and making notes on the map. "Come on," he said, "we need to re-evaluate the plan. Let's get back to our plane."

Later, he couldn't rest, tossing and turning, anxious about the smoke and what might be there waiting for them. The night seemed to last forever and the reavers' drone was clear, though somewhere in the distance, probably devouring another victim – something he didn't want to think about right then. However, he was glad the boy slept soundly – he needed his batteries recharged. His eyes rolled beneath their lids. Dreaming. Boucher wished he knew of what.

At dawn, they set out in the direction of the smoke. It had vanished from the skyline but Boucher had mapped its location the best he could. His spirits were up, and he kept reminding himself that there was no smoke without fire. And, more importantly, fire played a key role in surviving the Arctic.

They trekked on, the only sound their laboured breaths in rhythm with the crunching snow beneath them. He stopped the boy when he realized the ground level had changed – a slope hidden among the great white, dipping before them into a large valley.

Was this here the whole time and I never saw it?

It didn't matter. What did was the source of the smoke. They sat on a ridge near the top, overlooking the vast, u-shaped valley, framed by sheets of grey rock. Then the sun glinted off something – possibly steel – reflecting its rays skyward.

"Look," the boy said.

"I see it."

"What is it?"

"Can't tell from up here. Could be a Basler, like ours."

"Can we go see it, Dad?"

"Yes."

Their descent into the valley was slow

but didn't seem difficult, probably due to adrenaline or excitement, maybe both. Even the boy moved across frosty rocks with the sure-footedness of a mountain goat. The snow at the bottom was deeper than on the plain they'd left, making it tougher for them to navigate their way towards the gleam.

A short time later, Boucher pulled up, unable to feel his toes. To protect the boy, he hoisted him up onto his shoulders and struggled forward, until the faint smell of burning stopped him in his tracks. Not the warmth of a wood-burning campfire he'd hoped for, but the reek of rubber and fuel. Notions of supplies or survivors spurred him forward. He let Rémy down and they continued on.

"Dad, it is like our plane!"

The boy was right. It wasn't obvious at first, but with every step closer, it became clear that they were approaching the remains of a BT-67 – just like his plane, lying at the end of a deep snow trail.

He warned the boy not to get close and, to his surprise, he listened. The remnants of a tyre, along with warm embers, lay in what looked to be a man-made fire a few feet from the plane... which provided the boy an opportunity to remove his footwear and heat his feet. Boucher ordered him to stay put while he investigated the wreckage.

His mind pondered many scenarios, the bitter cold making it hard to think straight. A mass of scratches and scraps scarred the paintwork. Not the result of gravity forcing a steel bird into the ground. Unnatural, yet natural – evidence of a hellish incident. Judging by the positioning of the fuselage, he reckoned the pilot tried to crash land only for it to go wrong, as it often does.

Did reavers take this out of the sky during the day? They only come at night?

The cockpit window had smashed inward, and when he looked in, he had to turn away to steady himself. A body sat strapped in its seat, the burnt remains close to frozen. He held his breath as he climbed in, but the stench of charred human proved too much and he vomited bile out of the window.

"Dad?"

"I'm okay. Stay where you are." He wiped his chin and spat into the snow.

It was possible that the pilot had died before burning up. At least, he hoped that was the case. Though he wasn't surprised, he was still horrified to find more of the crew on the floor behind the seats – their flesh torn off in chunks to reveal bone.

Reavers take no prisoners.

He was mindful of sundown approaching. The fire hadn't burnt everything and, behind the cockpit, the cargo area seemed to be intact. With force, he managed to open the door and, again, struggled with a range of smells – none of them good. The boy called again, but he ignored him. Two unburnt bodies lay still on the floor. A man and a woman. He took a quick look around, then examined them. The man, in a pool of frozen blood, had a gaping stab wound in his neck. Probably caught shrapnel during the crash and bled out.

The woman was curled on her side and he rolled her over. Young, pretty, reminding him of the boy's mother. He stroked her face, pushed back some hair.

Then she groaned.

She's alive!

"Rémy!" he yelled. "Come here and help me."

He placed two fingers on her neck, finding a weak pulse, her breathing slow, but alive nonetheless. When he opened her jacket, her blood-soaked t-shirt clung to her skin. He examined her, finding a large chunk of steel wedged between her ribs.

Crap.

Behind him, the boy grunted and groaned as he climbed into the cockpit.

"Dad?"

"Don't be scared."

"But, they're dead…"

"The dead can't hurt you."

The boy's eyes widened, filling with terror at the scene before him. Boucher advised him to ignore the smell and focus on the woman.

"Who is she?"

"I don't know."

"Is she dead like the others?"

"No."

"Can we help her?"

"We're going to try."

He searched the cargo hold for something to transport her, with no luck. Eventually, using a sheet of material pulled from the aircraft's interior wall, they laid her out. It took great effort to open the damaged cargo door, lift her up, and carry the weighted stretcher outside. The boy struggled with the task, forcing Boucher to dive deeper into his reserve to set her down without letting her fall. He taught the boy how to tie a bowline hitch, which secured the woman for transport.

"Can we bring her back to our plane, Dad?"

"Yes. It's not safe here and this plane isn't set up for night-time like ours."

"How far away are we?"

"About three hours, I reckon."

"When will it get dark?"

"In about three hours..."

They waded out through the valley and across the white plains. With tremendous effort, they evaded crevices and struggled through soft snow, eventually making it back to their plane before dark, too exhausted to celebrate. Boucher was sure he felt the onset of frostbite but he was too afraid to look. The visual in his head would be enough to make him scream, so, instead, he opted to ignore the throbbing boot.

The boy looked concerned but said nothing, turning his attention to the woman laid out on the floor.

"Is she going to die, Dad?"

"I don't know," he replied, slow-dripping water on to her lips. A third mouth to feed, if she ever woke up – a concern he didn't feel guilty about. She wouldn't have stood a chance if they'd left her.

Exhaustion forced the boy into deep sleep – one without terrors, which Boucher was grateful for, allowing the night to pass in silence.

In the morning, he walked out and

broke the layer of ice over the boreholes and went about fixing the fishing lines. He stood watching the water ripple back into cold stillness before developing a thin layer of ice. As the days went by, the lake froze quicker and thicker, forcing his stomach to growl as he hungered for a quick catch.

To the east, the sun seemed to be higher than he was used to seeing during his routine. Perhaps he'd slept late? It was hard to tell. Every time he thought he had it figured out, a couple of days of cloud cover would come along and disorientate him. His foot had stopped throbbing, becoming more of a dull ache – a feeling he'd ignored for too long.

The air in the fuselage reminded him of a walk-in freezer. Still, it was warmer inside and that was all that mattered. The boy was still sound asleep, looking at peace, and he couldn't help but smile, probably the only thing that gave him joy in this dead world. He stepped over him, and the woman, as he made his way to the rear of the plane.

He sat on the toilet in the small lavatory and locked himself in. It hurt to remove his boots, the pain bolstered by his apprehension. To his horror, a mix of bloody blisters and blue-grey flesh greeted him, and he grimaced when his foot reacted to the chilled air – like raw nerve ends coming to life.

Fuck.

Biting down on his collar, he forced himself to examine the damage. Blackened crust had formed beneath his middle toes, probably between second and third degree – he couldn't be sure. However, he was certain he wouldn't be able to walk far in this condition.

'Frozen in January, amputate in July' – an old adage his squad leader used to repeat. He watched vapour rise from his mouth. *Will I even be alive in six months?*

A fasciotomy would help the swelling – that much he was sure of, but all he had at his disposal were some bandages, his pocket knife, and a couple of antiseptic wipes. Not enough to carry out a proper procedure.

41

The other plane might have something. He cursed himself for leaving in such haste. Then the harsh reality of his situation hit him. To be able to take care of the boy – and the woman – he would first need to take care of himself. And the only way he could do that was to deal with the frostbite here and now.

On his first attempt, he couldn't control the shaking – a mix of cold and dread – eventually giving up.

He took a few more minutes to gather himself, breathing slow and deep, psyching himself up with every exhalation. Then he removed his belt, folded it over, and placed it between his teeth.

Take two...

At first, an instant release warmed his foot as the pressure popped in a plume of blood, giving him a temporary moment of relief before the agony kicked in. He growled as his jaw tightened behind his gritted teeth, his tongue hard against the roof of his mouth. Sweat beaded on his forehead as he drove cool steel through flesh – blood and pus pouring over his hands. It took real effort to control his breathing – even more to keep his groans in check as he forced the blade through each joint, the snapping sound reminding him of a chicken wing being pulled apart.

Two toes hit the floor with a lifeless thud.

He leaned back, pulling his mangled foot as close into him as he could, staring at the ceiling as he squeezed – concentrating on his breathing while he fought every urge to scream. All he could do was hope and pray for sepsis to stay away.

The wind was strengthening outside, increasing the chill-factor, if that was possible in such a cold, barren place. When he emerged, the boy was waiting in the cargo hold, dressed and alert – worried. His moaning must have woken him.

Then he smiled. "Are you okay, Dad?"

"I'm fine, son. I think..."

"You sure?"

He jacked up his eyebrows and

43

shoulders, keeping his weight off his foot. "Yep."

The woman hadn't moved all night, and he feared she'd passed, but then he located a pulse. Still weak but steady. He trickled water on to her lips, then unzipped her sleeping bag and patted her legs, checking for soilage. Nothing. The chunk of steel protruding from her ribs appeared to stop any external bleeding. Internal might be a different matter. He searched on, finding only dry coldness. Then he found a wallet in her trouser pocket.

Working through his pain, he sat himself on the side-facing seats and opened it. The cracked leather housed only an ID badge, branded with *Ziegler Ecological Research Operations* in blue lettering. That was all. For now, the woman remained nameless.

The boy didn't take kindly to the news, but Boucher insisted on going south alone this time. The woman's plane could have essentials. This was important and a possible turning point in their quest for survival.

Rémy offered to help carry things, but Boucher eventually convinced him to stay and watch the woman and enjoy bonus playtime with his toys.

"When will you be back?" he asked.

"As soon as I can."

"But it's not bright yet?"

"I think this is as bright as it's going to get."

"What about them things?"

"Hopefully they only like pitch black. Stay inside and be quiet."

He looked at the wide-eyed boy, who stared back, his gaze blank. Even though he wasn't sure if he fully understood the situation, he still assured him everything would be all right. He wrapped up well, limped across the fuselage, and warned the boy to stay warm and hydrated in his absence. As he exited through the cargo-bay door, he told his son he loved him, then closed the door and headed into the dull white.

During his walk, he tried to distract himself from the pain. If things weren't so dire, the view was almost a sight to behold. He soldiered on, limping, resting – pushing forward – until he reached the ridge. His descent into the valley was tricky, but he managed to navigate the deep snow easier without the boy in tow.

He figured he had enough time to carry out a good search, gather whatever he could find, and make it back to base before total dark. It would be tough but it had been a long time since any sort of windfall came his way, and this drove him forward despite the pain and cold.

The plane was the same make and model as his – a common aircraft operating around the Arctic. Its structure had been fatally compromised on impact, ruling out any possible repair – he doubted there was anything salvageable, anyway.

A few things he'd missed the day before caught his attention, which he put down to exhaustion. Something he hadn't missed, because it wasn't there before, was the snow around the craft displaying a mass of paw tracks. They looked fresh enough, leading from the cargo door around to the far side of the plane.

Something wasn't right, and his scalp prickled as he stood still. The wind had died, leaving an eerie silence, broken by his heartbeat in his ears, like drumming from a marching band.

A noise from the far side stilled his breathing – a sound that could never be forgotten once heard: the frenzied gnashing of a feasting pack.

Wolves.

Unable to move as fear gripped every part of him, he surveyed the area and convinced himself that the safest place was inside the Basler. Then several of the beasts scurried into view, yelping and snapping at each other, their behaviour demonstrating a competitiveness inherent in those who'd landed a score of a lifetime.

He forced himself to move, hobbling towards the plane – in plain sight – vulnerable and terrified, blessed that the wolves were distracted enough to allow him slip away undetected to the front of the plane, where he dragged himself up and through the shattered windscreen.

Once inside, he eased the cockpit door shut, then released a sigh of relief and took time to catch his breath.

Outside, wolves feasted on the remains of the frozen crew members, their bodies having been dragged from the plane. He listened, waiting – hoping, once satiated, no interest would be taken in him.

A rank aroma filled the air, and he had to push the fear down as he recognised it. Composure was key. He studied the sky. Daylight seemed to be disappearing quicker now – he'd never make it back before dark. He glanced around. *There must be something... Anything.* He'd seen the crates before closing the cockpit door. He wanted to bust them all open but resisted the urge for fear of the wolves. Instead, he sat on the floor and waited in the biting cold.

Weary legs and a throbbing foot forced him to lay down, his eyelids heavier with each blink. The pack would leave before dark, he was sure of that. They wouldn't have survived this long if they hadn't adapted otherwise.

The boy was probably worried sick. Then a depressing thought hit him – it would be his first ever night alone. He hadn't given it sufficient thought, bent on the prospect of fresh supplies. Poor Rémy would be terrified. A single tear rolled down his cheek, until it was whipped away by the back of his hand.

He reached inside and pulled on a piece of cord tied around his neck, a white-gold ring on the end of it, engraved with initials and a date from the world he'd left behind. His mind went to *her* and the night they had to leave St. John's. Post-dusk had become deadly. Anything that moved when the sun was down instantly regretted it, and with the night taken from them, it didn't take long for daytime to become just as lethal. Society, it seemed, was always seconds from descending into anarchy.

Despite the chaotic streets, he brought the boy to the hospital, admiring the young lad's courage. While wandering the empty corridors, Rémy displayed a strength Boucher hadn't seen. Un-phased by a lingering scent of death, he showed an ability to ignore the cries from doomed souls in the wards. When they entered her room, she lay withered and alone, with all electronic equipment surrounding her powered down. If he'd known the sick would be abandoned so easily, he would have brought her home. Or tried. He assumed the boy got his courage from her – *an important trait that may stand to him someday*. How he'd wished for an ounce of it there and then. Watching mother and son embrace tore his heart, and saying goodbye to the woman he loved was the hardest thing he'd ever had to do.

He woke to the sound of the wind, with dawn creeping in through cracks in the wreckage. His first thoughts were of the boy. He had to get back. Bearing the pain in his foot, he scrambled to his feet and looked outside to see nothing but lifeless white in every direction, with random snow flurries whipped up from the wind.

With haste, he opened the cockpit

door and began looking in the crates, finding, for the most part, nothing but useless research documentation. After a while, though, the search produced results as he came across gas for a cooking stove, a first-aid box, several cans of processed food, and even an adult-size stretcher.

Adrenaline fuelled his eagerness, helping him ignore hunger and cold – he couldn't wait to offer the boy a warm meal. He loaded the stretcher with everything he could, turning it into a makeshift sled. With one last trawl, he stumbled upon a black crate hidden beyond the cargo area, beside the lavatory, its contents secured by a padlock. He struggled with the weight as he dragged it outside. Using a length of steel pulled from the wreckage, it didn't take long to snap the lock and pry the crate open. He couldn't believe his eyes on seeing the rifle and box of ammunition – his first thought went back to how he could have used it on the bear, instead of summoning reavers, who no doubt were now nesting in the vicinity.

Beneath the gun, he found a map, the discovery evoking a laugh of joy. He brought it inside and opened it out on the floor, comparing it to his hand-drawn effort. To his surprise, his mental map was accurate enough, except he didn't know where in the world he was jotting down. The map detailed outposts and research bases all around the Arctic Circle.

Comparing the limited features of the land, he was relieved to find that heading south-west would have led them to the fjord and across to the research outpost.

With a new sense of hope, he got his stuff together and made his way back to the boy, the loaded rifle strapped to his back.

He was greeted with a loving embrace from his son. Exhausted from hauling the sled across the snow-heavy tundra, all he could do was ask him if he was okay. However, the boy just cried tears of relief at his return. He wanted to cry, too, as he held him close.

"I'm sorry," he whispered, arms

trembling from strain and fatigue.

Rémy didn't reply and, eventually, Boucher said, "It'll be dark soon. Help me get this stuff inside."

They settled in for the night, finding homes for each item from the improvised sled. He checked the woman. No change, still breathing. He was eager to cook some of the canned food but noticed the boy couldn't take his eyes off the gun.

"It may come in useful," he said.

"Can I have a go?"

"Maybe tomorrow. For now, help me over here. You need to eat something."

He emptied the contents from the can of pasta into the saucepan and asked the boy what he ate while he was gone. His lack of response sparked an unwanted vision of him standing around, helpless – starving away.

"You need to start taking care of yourself, Rémy. I won't be around forever."

The boy remained silent, gazing at his figurines.

Boucher's heart ached as he wondered how he would survive the harshness of the new world alone.

"Here, try this." He scooped warm pasta onto his plate.

"What's the red stuff?"

"Try it. It's good."

"I don't like the look of it."

"It's just pasta in tomato sauce."

His eyes shadowed by a frown, he gave it a go, and, with loud slurps, he cleared the plate in seconds, his stomach growling.

"Can I have more?"

"Yes."

They woke during the night to the sound of screaming. The boy called out, while Boucher scrambled around looking for his torch. With a click, the LED blub lit up the fuselage. Rémy crawled towards the light and grabbed hold, while Boucher scanned the interior. The screaming got louder and more frantic as the woman shifted and convulsed.

"Make her stop, Dad. *They're* going to hear her."

Boucher shared the same concern. He scrambled across the floor and grabbed a firm hold of the woman's shoulders, but his touch seemed to add an extra layer of terror to her screams. He begged her to be quiet; however, her eyes looked through him as if he wasn't there. Then she clawed at his arms and he shifted around behind her, pulled her into him, his hand clamped over her mouth. He whispered in her ear, begging her to relax, assuring her that everything was all right.

The boy knelt in front of her, shushing, pleading with her to be quiet. Her eyes locked on his, and maybe it was the innocence, or fear – whatever she saw in him, caused her to stop struggling.

Boucher continued to whisper in her ear, calming her into silence before removing his hand.

"Are *they* coming, Daddy?"

"I don't know."

They lay on their blankets, hearts pounding. He held the boy and listened. Occasionally, the woman would whimper, and he'd hush her, knowing she was confused and terrified. But there was no time to explain everything right now.

Commotion was potentially lethal after dark and she had caused a lot of it. He prayed that the silence would continue, but to his despair, a faint droning came from beyond the walls.

"Make one sound and I'll have to kill you," he whispered to the woman.

She did not reply.

They lay there, listening to the screeching and scraping on the plane's exterior as flutters of rage from the creatures of the night forced cold sweat down their backs.

Rémy trembled in terror against Boucher, and, with no other choice, they lay awake in absolute silence, listening to the screeching and scraping until dawn.

"We can't stay here," he said to the boy.

"But I don't want to go."

"We have enough supplies to make the journey south. We have the map. I know where we're going. We can load everything on the sled. It'll take us about two days—"

"I don't want to go, Dad!"

His heart broke for the child, seeing

the genuine fear in his eyes. The trek would not be easy on him – on any of them – and with the weather getting colder, and after the night before, he was certain reavers would be close by, leaving little room for error regarding noises after dark.

Nevertheless, what choice did they have? Daylight had reduced to around six hours of nautical twilight, placing them around November, but he couldn't be sure, and months and time didn't matter anymore. The priority now was getting the boy to the research station in the south.

He offered the woman some water but she refused. When he spoke to her, she did not reply. He moved away to check supplies and the boy tried talking to her, but met the same stone-cold silence.

"You need to eat, lady," he said. Still no response. She hadn't eaten in days and her wound could become infected. In her current condition, she wouldn't last the journey south.

After he went back to helping the boy load the stretcher, the woman finally broke her silence. "Mister... I... agree with your boy. I don't want to leave here, either."

The morning had slipped past almost without notice. He studied her wound. A thick layer of crusty pus cracked when the dressing was removed. He touched the steel, which evoked a wince from her. Using alcohol wipes from the first-aid box, he dabbed around it and applied a clean dressing. It was the best he could do.

She drank warm water and ate a small amount of pasta, after which a flush of colour returned to her face. He pointed to their location on the map, then tapped on their destination. "We can't stay here and we have to go there."

"What's the point?" she asked, her accent carrying a German tone.

"No sunlight in winter. This wreck will be a tomb soon."

She pondered that for a moment, shifting herself upward. "The world is a tomb."

"What do you mean?"

"The media reported those... things on every continent."

"Are you serious? How do you know?"

"They said it was sort of a Black Swan event... No arsenal or weapon could do anything to prevent those things from spreading. By the time we tried to act, it was too late. Humanity never stood a chance..."

Boucher told the boy to go outside and watch the boreholes. He wasn't sure if the woman was unwell and rambling or telling the truth. But whatever she had to say, he knew the boy didn't need to hear it.

He waited, watching through the window as he went over to the boreholes. A sadness hit him, and he was sorry for the lost little soul.

"Were you stationed up here?"

"Yes."

"You guys tried to flee, didn't you?"

"Yes."

He showed her the map and pointed to where he believed her plane had come down. Before hope built inside of her, he revealed that she was the sole survivor. At first, she seemed okay with the news, then a single tear rolled down the side of her face. The sight of it stirred something in him – maybe it was the despair in her voice, or the void of hopelessness in her eyes. Either way, he was sure he felt it, too, resigning their fate to certain doom. It was only a matter of time.

"What's your name?" he asked.

"Zeigler. Matilda Ziegler."

Another night passed without incident and they set out on their daily routine. Somewhere behind grey clouds, sunlight struggled to break through.

They wandered in silence.

The boy carried a cup of warm water, sipping as he went.

Boucher did not speak. Deep inside, his heart ached as a wave of depression cloaked his mind.

When they reached the foot of the hill, he had to stop – his feet aching – the ascent looking more daunting than usual. He waited for the boy to catch up, pondering on where they could go from here, eventually concluding that this would be the last time the beacon would omit a signal.

"Why have we stopped?" Rémy asked.

"No reason." He took a deep, cold breath and let out a long sigh. "There's little reason for anything anymore..."

It was a windless day, much to their relief, as they sat on top of the hill listening to the beacon. He charged the device, the radio struggling to locate a signal. With the volume lowered, static no longer bothered him.

The boy watched wide-eyed as he dug away the snow beneath it.

He released another sigh, this one of relief, as he uncovered a frozen bottle of whiskey. Rémy smiled, mirroring his own reaction. It was probably the happiest the kid had seen him in a long time.

"What's that, Dad?"

"A special treat," he answered, watching his confused expression as he tucked the bottle into his coat. Then he told him that this treat needed to be warmed up before it could be enjoyed.

The boy still didn't get it. How could he? Little did he realize that an end game was being prepared for – there was nothing left in the world for them other than waiting for a slow, cold, hungry death.

About an hour later, the plastic seal broke with a satisfying crack. Boucher gulped down a mouthful and relished the burn flowing through his chest. He wasn't a religious man but, right there and then, he secretly thanked God and asked for a sign – something to validate his thoughts; dark musings involving the killing of the woman and the boy. Mercy kills, before overcoming his abhorrence for suicide.

What other choice did he have?

God's mysterious ways were allowing them to either starve to death, freeze to death, or wait for the new dominant species to devour them. If this was all part of some divine plan, he decided that he was more than prepared to face the consequences for doing God's work.

The lad doesn't deserve to suffer. He's had no part in the horrors that changed the world at such a rapid pace, robbing his generation of a future. No, he's seen enough horror at such a young age. I can't let him suffer anymore. Quick and painless is the only way. It's my right as his parent. And, God, if you can hear me now and have a problem with it, then all I can say is...fuck you.

"Come on, son, let's head back to camp."

Within the static, a faint voice revealed itself. At first, he couldn't be sure, but when the boy got excited, they both dashed over and raised the volume. The signal was scrambled, but something came through the white noise – a crackly voice, saying the same words over and over, like an announcement or broadcast, in different languages. They listened, huddling in close. The first round was English, then it changed to what he believed was Nordic.

...name is Jürgen Ziegler... ...this is an emergency broadcast... ...if you can hear this, you are not alone... ...we are scienti... ...can offer shelter at our research fac... ...ZERO... ...travel in small groups during daylig... ...stay silent... ...our coordinates

```
are-
```

A wall of static filled the beacon's tiny speaker.

"Dad?"

"Quiet. There's more. Listen…"

```
…latitude 68-
```

A flurry of static consumed the recording again.

```
…longitu-
```

Boucher hit the beacon in frustration and the boy offered a calming hand on his shoulder. They waited and eventually managed to decipher the full message.

He studied his map while the boy continued to listen to the broadcasts.

"I think I know which station he's referring to."

"Really?"

"Yes."

The boy watched him. "What are you doing?"

"Praying."

"Why?"

"To give thanks for the sign…"

"You need to tell me about the station in the south," Boucher demanded, dropping everything as he entered the plane.

"What?" Matilda replied, startled and struggling to get upright.

He didn't care, kneeling in front of her, looking her in the eye. "The research station. Your plane took off from there, didn't it?"

"What makes you say that?"

He told her everything: the map, the recording, and the scientist by the name of Jürgen. But the one detail he focused on was the surname: Ziegler.

The woman sighed, leaning over on her side. She looked at the boy, then at Boucher, then to the lump beneath her clothing where the steel fused into her ribcage. "We'll never make it that far. Not in our condition."

"We can't stay here, Matilda. What's the deal?"

"Jürgen is my husband. He sent me and some of the team away when the outbreak went into full swing. Besides, you said it was a recording, they could all be dead by now."

"True. However, staying here is a death sentence. If they are dead, the facility may still have something to offer. We need food and medical supplies..." He let his sentence hang, gazing at the woman and the boy with undisguised hope.

With no other choice, she gave him a slight nod and no more.

Boucher prepared a meal for three using up the last of their canned pasta and fish. They ate in silence, the adults finishing the whiskey. He couldn't help but feel as if it was some sort of last supper. The booze offered slight relief but, every once in a while, his concerns for the boy flooded his thoughts. Was the woman right? Was this a march into certain death? Was the facility now a ruin? If they survive the journey, what dangers would await them? All the uncertainty made him – a man of routine – uncomfortable. He placed his hand on the boy and told him he loved him.

"My plane crashed here some time ago," Boucher said, breaking the silence as he looked at the woman. She did not reply, looking back at him instead, as if waiting for him to continue.

"The creatures ravaged everything. Cities and towns burned. I had to get my boy out of danger."

She slurped up a piece of pasta. "You can fly a plane, Mister?"

"The name's Boucher. Jeremy Boucher. And this is my son, Rémy. I used to be with the Canadian Rangers. And, yeah, I can fly a plane. Went freelance after the Range—"

"Like an ice pilot?" she interrupted.

"Yeah, running supplies around the Arctic in this bird for science folk like you. We left St. John's—"

"And made the mistake of flying during the night?" she interrupted again.

"Yeah... thought we could get across to Scotland or Norway, but needed a stopover for refuelling on the way. So, I took us north, towards Greenland. Was planning on setting down in Nuuk but those things attacked. Lost my sense of direction. Still... managed to get her down, despite the dark."

The woman pondered his story. "In

my line of work, I've come across several ice pilots. Tough job." She shifted again until she found a spot she could tolerate. "My team and I were fleeing for Canada. We learnt fast that those things hunt at night, but not over sea. As soon as we were over land, they swarmed us in a black fog."

"You come from Europe, right?"

"Originally, yes. We were stationed at the ZERO."

"The ZERO?"

"Yes... my husband's transmission... the coordinates..." Her voice tapered off.

"What happened there? Why did you run?"

She didn't answer.

"Matilda... why did you flee?"

"Jürgen and I had a disagreement... He wanted to stay. And the rest of us wanted to leave."

"So, he set up the broadcast?"

"Probably to get other research stations to join him."

"Why? What was so important?

The woman began coughing, her voice

turning raw and raspy. "Well, the last thing we heard was that *they* came from somewhere along the Arctic tundra. My colleagues guessed melting of permafrost was the cause—"

"Of what?"

"The reavers..."

Boucher didn't reply. He looked to the boy, who hung on the woman's every word.

"Before we knew it," she continued, "reports came in of cities being overrun, like a plague from the bible. Daylight offered respite... allowing millions to flee, but soon—"

"Humanity revealed its true self?"

"Yes. Yes, it did." She winced, clutching her chest.

He slumped back against the wall and let out a loud sigh, not wanting to talk anymore. His thoughts brought him back to the streets and the quick collapse of civilized society. Humans had become more dangerous than the creatures of the night.

Maybe God had a plan after all.

When morning broke, Boucher and the boy woke to the sound of screaming. In their confused state, it took them a moment to realize that it wasn't from fear, but agony.

The woman had left her blankets and was curled into a foetal position in the middle of the fuselage. Her nails dug into her legs and her screams turned to whimpers, then to howls, and back to whimpers.

Boucher rushed to her aid. Her skin had raised in a bright-red blister around her wound, reminding him of a volcano, only instead of lava in its crater, a dull green pus oozed from beneath the cracks in the scabbing.

"Dad?" The boy stared, terrified of the sight before him.

"It's badly infected. She needs a doctor."

"Will the monsters come tonight if they hear her?"

"We can't stay here any longer," he answered as he tried to calm the woman. He held her close, keeping his voice soft in an effort to ease her breathing. When she quietened, he let out a frustrated sigh. "No more excuses, son. Start packing... essentials only. We have to leave today."

The boy stared at the vast whiteness outside the window, his shoulders dropping before he went to gather his belongings.

The woman groaned and tensed, and Boucher held her hand until she passed out from whatever was going on inside her. In his mind, he was convinced the research facility would have something that could help her. *God would not have sent me a message otherwise. This is our purpose. Our only hope.*

They gathered up essentials for the trek across the bitter landscape – mostly clothing and the rifle.

He changed the dressing on his foot and was thankful to God again for not seeing infection where his toes had been.

The boy was dressed and ready to go – his eyes wide and fearful.

As Boucher strapped the woman to the sled, she woke, mumbling, as if delirious. He kept his voice low and soft as he explained that getting to the research facility was their only hope of survival.

"There... is nothing... We can't—"

"Quiet," he begged, then a cold gust of wind greeted them as the cargo door slid open. "We can't stay here. I'm taking us to the ZERO," he announced and began pulling the sled out into the wild.

PART TWO
ASCENSION

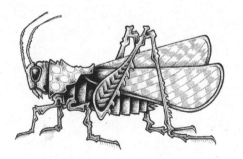

PART TWO
ASCENSION

They trudged on in the pale light that passed for day. Over harsh terrain, the sled seemed to get heavier as time went by, and Boucher often had to stop for rest and water. At least that was how it felt. In reality, he knew his body was fading. His hands shook as he struggled to steady his cup, and the boy asked if he was okay. He grunted a reply and studied the map. Somewhere in the distance, an animal, probably a bird, sounded off. He figured it was in response to the dark cloud looming in the direction they were going.

"Are we close?" the boy asked.

He showed him the map and dragged his finger along it. They were heading for a range of hills that would take them down towards the ocean. "If we get to the coast, our trek should be easier."

"I'm cold."

"I know. We'll shelter when we reach the hills."

"Okay."

They moved south through the knee-deep snow. The dark clouds were over them now and their daylight was fading at a rapid pace. Boucher reckoned they were heading into a storm but, as they got closer, he feared it might be worse – a blizzard. Swirls of snow lifted from the ground in the quickening wind.

"We need to hurry," he said.

Within minutes, the temperature plummeted and he ordered the boy to cover up; an Arctic blizzard could freeze the face within seconds. Visibility became difficult as the storm kicked in. He dragged the sled with all his might, scanning the rocks for an opening large enough to provide shelter. With his energy depleted, he ordered the boy ahead. Rémy responded without protest, no doubt fully aware of the threat against them.

To Boucher's joy, the boy found a large crack in the snow-covered rock face. However, the sled was too large to fit through the entrance, forcing him to remove the woman and drag her inside, after he'd taken the rifle and scouted the space for the likes of a sheltering polar bear. Wind howled outside as total whiteout froze everything it touched. The cave was small, just about offering a safe place to ride out the storm.

"Dad?" the boy called.

He didn't reply at first, holding him close instead, huddled against the back wall. "We'll be safe in here. Just need to keep warm."

They watched the snow drift at the entrance until it sealed them in, the darkness adding weight to the bone-deep cold.

Later, he was half-asleep when a noise snapped him awake. It happened again and he sat up, patting the cold ground until he touched the boy. They must have dozed off. More noise. He flicked on his torch and shook the boy. "Wake up."

"What is it?" he asked, wiping his eyes.

Boucher had no answer nor any sense of the time. A rustling came from beyond the wall of snow. He lifted the rifle and fingered the safety, his hand shaking. "There's something outside."

"Dad?" the boy whispered, his voice laced with fear.

"Quiet."

He crawled over to the entrance and listened, his eyes closed as he focused. Nothing. He listened again, then, using the barrel, poked a hole in the snow at the top, until he saw a clear night sky. Stars twinkled and a bright moon lit up the fresh snow that blanketed the landscape. The blizzard had passed. His gut clenched at a nearby noise – different, though, to what he expected from the creatures. This was more *natural*, like animals communicating with each other in low yelps and growls. The sled had been pulled apart. Scavengers, looting their supplies.

Must be the same pack from the woman's aircraft. They have a taste for human flesh.

That thought rattled him – all that separated them from the wolves was a thin layer of snow. He signalled to the boy to be quiet, hoping the pack would lose interest and move on.

"Dad?"

"I said be quiet."

"Dad, look..."

The woman was shifting under her blankets. He knew what was coming next, and dropped the rifle but, before he could get over to her, she screamed.

He scooped up her bedding and draped himself in it. Too late, a snout broke through the snow, followed by three sets of golden eyes. He lunged forward and turned, blocking the entrance with his back.

Rémy pleaded with the woman to be quiet, but she seemed to get louder, gripping the steel protruding from her ribs.

The growling became intense as the wolves snapped and fought with each other, their leader biting and dragging at Boucher. He roared as loud as his lungs would allow as its jaws ripped through the layers, niggling away at his flesh.

"Dad!" the boy screamed.

He looked up to see the boy standing in front of him, rifle in hand.

"No!" he shouted. "Don't shoot. It'll only draw them..."

As if on cue, a droning came from somewhere outside – the wolves stopped nipping at him and he dropped to his knees, turning to look after them. They were nowhere to be seen. He crawled over to the woman and covered her in the torn blanket, begging her to be silent – her eyes showed that she was trying, though a wince escaped from her contorted mouth.

For a moment, he thought about

clamping his hands down over her nostrils and mouth, but she softened and slipped back into unconsciousness. No time to waste – he scurried over to the entrance, packed the snow back up as best he could, then pulled the boy under the blanket, listening to the wolves fighting helplessly against the night. The three of them stayed silent until morning.

When day broke, he pushed his way out of the cave and studied the scene. His back ached from the pounding he'd received from the wolves, but bruising and scrapes he could handle. It would have been so different if the bites had done the intended damage. From earlier observation, the gnaw marks looked superficial. He trudged out into the snow and examined the scattered supplies lying around the sled, then salvaged what he could. In the distance, track marks and bloodstains were visible. He called to the boy, who emerged from the slit in the rock, shivering.

"We have a long walk ahead and it's getting too dangerous. I don't know how we survived last night."

The boy stared at the wilderness, his eyes wide.

"Gather up your things. And go to the toilet, too. We won't be stopping once we get moving."

It surprised him that the lad didn't argue with him, going about retrieving what he could from the supplies and packing them into his rucksack. Then he took a piss on a drift and watched the stream rise up, disappearing into the air.

Boucher did what he had to do, basically the same as the kid.

"Dad?" the boy cried on seeing him trudge through the snow, carrying nothing but a rucksack.

"Come on, son. We need to leave."

"What about Matilda?"

"We've done all we can for her."

"What? No."

"Look, son, last night was too close a call. She is a liability. Next time, we might not be so lucky."

He stomped the snow. "I am not leaving her behind."

"There's nothing more we can do, son. Her infection – she's going to die."

"No. I'm not leaving *her* behind again."

Boucher's heart sank. Standing there in the vast nothingness, his boy scared, motherless, and lonely. Nevertheless, what choice did he have? Her screams could get them killed. He couldn't risk it. His boy was too precious to him. And with the facility within reach, the possibility of salvation during the winter was too close to be risked. He didn't argue anymore and walked on for about ten feet, then stopped and called the boy.

Rémy stood firm, his arms folded across his chest.

Anger boiled inside Boucher. The boy was stubborn and they didn't have time for this. His first impulse was to grab him and convince him that this decision was best for their survival. He took a step towards him and felt the loud crack just before he heard it. Everything went still for what seemed like an eternity. Then, in desperation, he called to the boy but, before any words came out, the snow swallowed him.

Boucher knew he wasn't dead when thoughts of days gone by flittered through his mind. He replayed the night in the hospital, and couldn't help but feel a deep sense of remorse at the sight of the boy's mother. Rémy had left the room and waited in the corridor. It was like he knew it was a last goodbye. Boucher kissed his wife and caressed her face with the back of his hand. His eyes teared up – outside, their world was ending.

"I can't leave you here like this, Vicky Bear," he said.

"There's nothing you can do," she replied, grimacing. "I have accepted my fate. The cancer chose me. All you have is the knife I got you for our anniversary, and it won't be enough to defend us against what's out there."

Fighting back tears, he looked out the window at a dying city.

He came to her side, held her hand, and gave a gentle squeeze. It had the texture of an eighty-year old – withered and frail.

Music played from the corridor. They looked to the door and saw the boy with a battery-powered speaker system in his hand – one of his mother's favourite songs playing.

She held Boucher's sleeve, her grip weak, and pulled him closer. "Everything we've ever known is gone. All that's left is him. Your job now is to get him away from this—"

"No!"

"Listen to me, Jeremy. The cancer has not eaten into my mind yet. I'm telling you now that if you stay, it won't be those *things* that kill you, it will be society."

He knew what she was talking about. He'd seen it already. Citizens attacking each other, with no sense of law and order. People he once called neighbours were now nothing more than threats. So many seemed to be beyond desperate. How could he argue with her? It didn't take long for reports of rape, murder, and even cannibalism to spread around the built-up areas.

"Jeremy, head north. Take your plane

and fly away from here."

The news had stopped broadcasting some time ago, as did social media. Parts of the city still had electricity but that commodity became a currency where only those willing to kill benefited.

"I can't leave you here."

"Jeremy..." She coughed. "I haven't been outside these four walls in months and even I know what's happening out there. As soon as the doctors fled and left me here, I knew that everything we've ever known is done. Please, take our boy away from this place."

"I can take you with us."

"Don't be silly, my love. You know as well I do, we missed that window of opportunity some time ago."

"Darling..." He lay his head in her open hand and let the tears flow. She ran her frail fingers through his hair for a minute or so before he sat up and wiped his eyes. "Okay."

In the hallway, he asked the boy to move away but to leave the music playing so he knew his location. It wasn't long before an unplugged version of Elton John's Rocket Man filtered up from the end of the corridor.

He turned to his wife and kissed her goodbye. Her final words *'I will always be with you'* forever etched in his mind as he opened her veins with his anniversary present.

Somewhere in his subconscious, Vicky's voice called to him, pleading with him to wake. When his eyes opened, everything swirled. He shook his head to clear his vision and take in his surroundings. Several metres above him, through a crack in the snow, the boy was hysterical, calling out to him, over and over. When he tried to move, a pain like no other shot through him, his screams echoing upwards.

He lay flat on his back at the bottom of the fissure, his right hip on a sharp grey rock protruding a few inches from the ground. Blood stained the snow around him.

"Dad!" the boy cried.

"I'm... okay," he lied, his voice

cracking. He was far from okay. And with the rock keeping his hip raised, he didn't have the strength to lift himself off it. His heart fluttered as a rush of panic flooded him. The boy was up there alone. If conditions worsened and he didn't get moving, the Arctic chill would kill him. Then the realisation of the boy being his only hope dawned on him.

He laughed. Cried. Laughed again. Then called to the boy, begging him to be calm and pay attention. "Listen carefully, son. Go back to the sled and gather all the straps and rope and bring them here."

The boy disappeared from view and he feared that might be the last time he'd see him. He tried to get up, but the slightest movement caused excruciating pain. There had to be something... Anything.

He looked around. Nothing but a slit in the earth – all ice and rock.

As he lay waiting for the boy to return, he tried to keep his circulation going by rotating his arms, hands, and feet. His boot brushed against something soft, and he raised himself up as far as the pain would allow. By his feet, strange black sacks lined the ground. He tipped them again – rubber-like, unfrozen and organic.

What the fuck?

"Hey, Dad, I'm back."

"Good job, son. Did you get the straps and rope?"

"Yeah."

"Okay, I need you to start tying them together. Remember the bowline hitch I thought you?"

"I think so..."

The boy grunted and groaned somewhere out of view and Boucher thought it best to leave him to it – he'd get it after a while. Then he appeared and signalled that everything was tied together.

Boucher asked him to look around for something on the surface to tie one end to and the boy disappeared from view again. When he reappeared, he lowered the line.

"What's it tied to?" He pulled the line hard, testing its strength.

"A big rock."

"Okay."

He looped the end of the rope around his wrists, took a deep breath, and began counting. On three, he pulled himself up – the pain was tremendous but the pressure from the rock eased beneath him. He paused for another breath, then pulled again. Without warning, the rope slackened and he slammed back down – his cry of agony filling the void above.

The boy called down to him.

Boucher struggled to catch his breath, sure he was about to pass out. But if that happened, all was lost. He managed to control his senses and slow his breathing enough to steady his thoughts. "I... I need you to tie it to the rock again. Triple-tie it this time, okay?"

"Okay."

He lay back, gathering his strength for the effort ahead. A squelching came from his hip wound. Shadows nudged at his vision and he slapped his face a few times to stay conscious – if he passed out now, he'd bleed out and that would be the end of it, for both of them.

When the line came back down, he

tugged and pulled it with as much force as he could muster. Satisfied that it would hold, he wrapped the line around his wrists as tight as he could. The rope dug in, breaking the flesh, but he didn't care – getting out of the hole was the only thing on his mind.

Pushing through the pain barrier was exhausting. Nevertheless, when he lifted himself off the sharp rock, moved to the side and plonked back onto the icy ground, a sense of victory washed over him. However, the pain pushed back. He untangled his hands and pressed blind on the wound. It seemed to be just a chunk of flesh above his hip that got it – a lucky escape. With his energy levels depleted, he called to the boy to let him know he was okay.

Using the rope, he struggled to his feet and looked up, figuring it was about three metres further to the opening. Not a massive climb but, in his condition, it would take everything he had. His body ached all over, and he was beyond tired. The cold numbed him but the pain overrode it. If it weren't for the boy, he would probably lie back and welcome whatever release came to him, even death.

The rope ate into his now-bloody wrists as he hoisted himself up. Even the intense cold couldn't cool the burn. He kept going, digging into what was left of his reserves, the boy calling for him not to give up.

When he reached the rim, he threw an elbow over, then his other, wedging himself with his legs, then gathered his breath and pulled himself out onto the snow. The boy did what he could to drag him away, before diving on him and squeezing, his face wet against Boucher's cheek.

They returned to the cave as fast as they could to get away from a freezing wind that had come out of nowhere. Inside, and to their surprise, the woman was awake, seemingly content with herself.

Boucher eased himself down at the back of the cave, then inspected his wounds.

The boy assisted as best he could,

clearly worried about his condition. As a distraction, he was ordered to pack up the entrance.

When the woman asked what happened, she got no reply.

Boucher concentrated as he ran his fingers over the gaping hole just above his hip. It was bad but, for some reason he couldn't explain, there was no pain. Maybe adrenaline? Shock? It didn't matter, it needed to be dressed to avoid infection.

The boy rummaged and gathered up what he could from their supplies, returning with the last of the medical stuff.

Using gauze, Boucher packed the wound and wrapped a tight dressing around it, then sank back against the wall, struggling to catch his breath. He looked at the woman. *Does she know I abandoned her?*

"Dad?"

"I'm okay, Rémy. Just need a little time." He struggled to catch his breath. "Help me clean these bite marks, will you?" The boy did as he was told, and Boucher winced as the abrasions were tended to.

The woman – fully awake now – watched them from her spot, her focus on him – on his face. "I don't blame you for leaving me behind, Jeremy."

"What?" he asked, pretending not to understand.

"You left me here to die."

"I didn't—"

"Don't lie." She shifted onto her side to get a better look at him. "I don't blame you. I would have done the same."

He did not reply.

"Anyway," she continued, "by the looks of things, we are both done for now, eh?" She pulled back the blanket to reveal her wound – oozing a bright-yellow pus – causing the boy to recoil in horror.

"I just need some... time to regain my strength," Boucher croaked. "I will get us to the ZERO." He fought for breath. "We have to keep... faith." He broke into a fit of coughing.

"Faith?" she said, ignoring his

struggle.

He spat away to the side. "Yeah..."

"If there is a God, he turned his back on this world a long time ago."

"Don't say that." He coughed and spat again. "Humanity will live on. We will persevere."

The woman shifted again and stared straight at him. "We have done this to ourselves."

"What do you mean?"

"No point hiding it anymore, is there, Jeremy? I never asked anything about you because I wasn't sure if I could trust you. What my team and I in ZERO are responsible for..." She looked at the cave entrance. "All of this."

"What are you talking about?" he asked, sitting up, giving her his full attention, the boy by his side.

She explained to them that the scientists in ZERO were contractors, tasked with drilling and fracking beneath the Arctic tundra. "We were warned about melting permafrost. Nevertheless, the committee pressed on. Our scientists said it was unethical when we started releasing toxins. The risks were high."

"Risks of what?"

"Well, for a start, ancient microbes and poisons. Doing what we were doing caused an anthrax outbreak a few years ago. There are old viruses and even risks of things like smallpox making a comeback from their prehistoric prisons. But the reality was, we couldn't have known what was frozen there. And how deadly the risk could have been..."

"Reavers?" the boy asked.

She nodded once, then took a deep breath and explained the discovery of a lifetime. Deep in the permafrost, something primordial had lain dormant for millennia. A form of insect larva that waited millions of years to hatch. "It all happened so fast. Once thawed, they multiplied and spread faster than anything we've ever seen before."

"My God," Boucher gasped.

She didn't reply, stiffening and twitching as her eyes rolled to the back of her head, passed out from the pain, and the poison spreading through her.

He looked to the boy. "Try to get some rest, son, we get moving at dawn."

Later, he lay listening to water dripping somewhere above the cave. His mind cast back to the floor of the fissure and the egg-like things he'd encountered. The creatures of the night had upset the natural order, exposing society's weakness in a matter of days – the resulting chaos turning people on each other.

"Are you okay, Dad?" the boy asked.

"This is not God's plan, son. We are the architects of our own downfall."

In the morning, Boucher was up and moving, checking outside to see a light snow flurry had left the area around the cave entrance powdered. The cold bit into him, and it took effort to get his circulation going enough to burn the blue from his fingers. Although struggling, he managed to redress his and the woman's wounds, and got the boy ready for the long trek ahead.

"Just leave me here to die," the

woman demanded. "I can't go back there. Jürgen will never forgive me for leaving."

"No."

"That's what you wanted, wasn't it? And it is best for you and your son. I will only slow you both down."

Boucher looked to the boy, who glared back wide-eyed and resolute. Nothing more needed to be said.

"Damn it, lady, your team should have listened to the warnings. Perhaps, then, this disaster could have been avoided. And I... should have listened to my boy. I'm not leaving you behind to die alone in the dark."

They spent the rest of the morning rebuilding the sled before heading towards the coast in the grudging light. Boucher stopped pulling the load every thirty or forty steps to have a coughing fit – each bout agonising – the freezing air stabbing into his lungs as his body convulsed.

The boy offered him water each time and they trudged on through the snow, soon picking up pace as the depth reduced, revealing a grey gravel-like surface. Buoyed by the changed landscape, Boucher redoubled his efforts and it wasn't too long before they came to a slope that led onto a brown rocky embankment.

He released a painful, yet joyous cry at the sight before them: a large frozen fjord, and across it, a structure that had no business among the Arctic wilderness.

"Is this where the man on the radio told us to go, Dad?"

"I believe so."

The woman shifted up onto her elbow. "We're here."

"It's getting dark," Boucher said, scanning the shoreline. "We have to cross now, before..." He looked to the boy, passed him his rucksack, and told him to stay close. And with everything he had left inside, he gripped the rope tight and dragged the sled across the fjord.

PART THREE
THE GREAT CESSATION

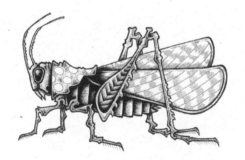

They crossed the fjord with caution, Boucher taking great care with every step. The sled seemed surprisingly light and, despite his limp, he managed to make good progress, the boy following with their bags. He sensed an apprehension in the lad, no doubt a fear of the unknown, or perhaps he didn't want to see hope die in his father's eyes again.

The ice made strange noises, as if in protest at them walking across it. Without warning, a large crack appeared beneath them, followed by what he could only describe as a pained groan as two large bodies of ice pushed and ground against each other.

"We have to hurry, it's becoming unstable."

With every step they took, ice weakened and more cracks shot in every direction, like a spider's web. Boucher pulled the sled and ordered the boy to move ahead of him. Behind them, chunks of ice broke away and sank below. Saltwater sprayed upward – he could taste it in the air. Only a few feet ahead, the boy climbed the bank onto iced dirt, then turned and shouted encouragement. The sled seemed heavier than ever now, the woman in a state of panic. *Almost there*. The cracks were shooting from each footstep and he struggled to maintain his balance. *We're going to go under.* The boy pleaded for him to hurry. Then, with a jolt, he came to a halt, pain burning into him from his hip wound.

"It's stuck!" the woman screamed.

He turned to see the sled wedged

between two large chunks of ice. Behind it, an open body of water expanded, sucking everything in its path under. Without hesitation, he grabbed the woman by her feet and pulled with all his might. In seconds, the sled disappeared from view. More ice split as the sea surged, coming for them. The woman and the boy screamed, and Boucher thought it was the end, but when he stepped back, pulling her with him, he landed at the boy's feet.

Beyond the rocky shore, roughly twenty metres away, a building was smothered in a white mist. Red corrugated walls made up the exterior of the long rectangular two-story building – its windows still intact. The structure was no doubt durable, even while it showed signs of exposure to the extreme elements this far north.

Boucher left the boy and the woman together and approached with hope of a warm welcome, but it seemed deserted. He walked around the complex. To the rear, smaller buildings came into view –

each flying a flag from different nations. Whoever was last stationed here had long gone. Did the broadcast attract others and they all fled?

He made his way back to the boy and woman. "More of a research village than station," he said.

The woman tried to reply but was overcome by a sudden onslaught of coughing. She clutched her ribs, gasping for breath between roars of pain.

In his mind, he knew without a hospital and a damn good surgeon, she was done for. All he could do was comfort her, as he'd done before. Ending her suffering was the easiest option, but the boy would never allow it – something he was mindful of. He took a deep breath and managed to lift her up, then nodded ahead. "We have to search the buildings."

"For what?" the boy asked.

"Anything that can help her. Medicine... alcohol. Come on."

They passed the red building and made their way down what appeared to be a main pathway. Corrugated-steel buildings framed each side of the gravel track. They were smaller than the main station, each a different colour: blue, red, yellow, dark green. At the far end, a large mast with rusted satellite dishes and a blinking red light rose above them. A weathered sign greeted them:

Welcome to
ZERO
Zeigler Ecological Research Operations

Hairs stood on the back of his neck. He hoisted the woman up into a more comfortable position. She was out again. The one time he needed her, she was no good to them. If she were awake, she could answer all his questions.

The buildings weren't marked, making it difficult to tell what could be inside each one. He asked the boy to look in the windows, and he reported back that he couldn't see anything.

"Are they empty inside?"

"No..."

"What do you see?"

"Wood."

"What?"

"Come see…"

He was in no mood for games but indulged the boy and looked inside the window of the first building. The kid was telling the truth – all he could see were wooden slats boarding up the window from the inside. When they checked more buildings, the result was the same. And all the doors were locked.

The woman shifted and her eyes opened. She looked around. "It's… deserted."

"Then why is that light blinking?" he asked, nodding to the mast. "I don't like the vibe I'm getting from this place."

"Me neither," the boy said.

He gave Rémy a half-smile. "That could be the source of Jürgen's transmission. Maybe it's running on a generator." He looked around and let out a long breath. "Why would he ask others to come to this place, only to lock up and leave?"

Boucher turned a full circle, deciding

which one to break into first. The boy sat on a step in a doorway, beside the woman, who lay where she'd been placed. He got up and approached a narrow path running between two buildings, his focus on something low down but out of Boucher's sight.

He didn't look for permission, just continued on, honing in on whatever held his fascination. Something in Boucher told him to follow, and a shiver shot through him when he looked around the corner to see a dried, bloodied trail that led to a pool of frozen guts on the ground at the end of the walkway. He quickened his pace, terrified of what lay ahead but not wanting to shout at the boy for fear of spooking him. Further on, human remnants, skint of flesh, lay scattered about the yard. The boy stopped dead in his tracks, arms by his sides, hands wide open.

"Don't look at them," Boucher said, standing behind him.

"Dad? What—"

He spun the boy around to face him.

"Don't you ever go wandering off again."

"But—"

"I don't care what excuse you have. We don't know this place."

The boy started to cry.

Boucher felt for him. As much as he tried to understand and see the kid's point of view, he knew he couldn't fully comprehend the potential dangers. He'd been through so much already, with the loss of his mother and normal life to those creatures. It wasn't fair to him. He gave the boy a hug, squeezed him tight, and wished for everything to be okay.

When they returned to the main walkway, the woman was where he'd left her, sitting with her back against the building. She was fading – her face pale like a waning moon, eyes sullen and deep. Without urgent medical attention, she was a goner.

They stepped forward in tandem and, in that instant, any sense of wind and cold disappeared as stones hopped up from the gravel track, followed by plumes of dust and debris. Through the haze, the woman, wide-eyed, signalled to them, her mouth open in a frozen scream. Then, somewhere in the distance, an echo broke the silence.

He knew the sound from long experience. Without thinking, he grabbed his son and rushed back between the buildings. The boy lay flat, blank-faced and wide-eyed.

Boucher unzipped his parka and checked him for wounds, relief coursing through him when he found none.

The boy's mouth worked, as if he was speaking, but no sound came. Then the dream-like slow motion ended when Boucher looked down at his own legs and saw the blood. Whoever was raining bullets down on them, had clipped him. He winced but moved in front of the boy to shield him.

Men were shouting out on the road. He told the boy to stay put, then crept up the side of the building and peeked around the corner in time to see an armed group marching down the street, firing off rounds at will. Three men. They could be soldiers, or a militia. Either way, they were trigger happy and looking for trouble. They gathered around the woman.

"Where are the others?" one of the men demanded. Boucher couldn't make out her reply.

"Dad?" the boy whispered.

"Quiet!"

Two of the men dragged her up and pulled her off towards the research station. He wanted to chase after her but knew it would be an exercise in futility. And now the boy was shaking. He tried comforting him, but he recoiled.

"I want to go back to the plane. I don't like it here. You told me it would be safe."

"Keep your voice down—"

"You said we would be okay. Why did you lie? Why did you lie to me?"

Boucher had no answer.

"What are those men going to do to her?"

"I don't know—"

"It was our job to help her. I want to go back to the plane."

114

He tried to hug the boy again, this time managing to wrap his arms around him. He struggled but he held him tight, whispering to him until he calmed.

"It's getting dark, son. We have to hole up somewhere before—"

"We have to save her, Dad."

He held the boy's shoulders. "For all we know, she's already dead."

"We can't leave her. You left her behind once and look what happened. I nearly lost you."

"Rémy—"

"No. You made me leave Mom. Not again. I can't..."

He tucked his head in against his chest and whimpered. Boucher released a quiet sigh. Here they were, lost and alone somewhere near Earth's frozen summit. Even if they wanted to leave, could they? They wouldn't last long in the wilderness – the journey so far had nearly killed them.

This was no time to think negatively. He shook his head clear – time to get a grip on the situation. If those men were soldiers, and stationed at the facility, surely they'd have supplies, or even transport. But none of that would matter if they were caught out in the dark.

From the far end of the laneway, something clicked, and he knew without looking that they'd been caught. He lifted his head to see a solider, his weapon aimed at them.

"Don't move."

Boucher raised his hands into the cold air.

Using his non-trigger hand, the solider pressed a button on a radio fixed to his lapel. Static followed before he spoke. "I found the rest of them, Major. Just off the main road. A man and a boy. Bringing them in now."

Three soldiers met them at the main entrance to the research station. Boucher noticed, as they were scrutinized from head to toe, that the men looked clean and well-fed – early signs that they'd come to the right place, aside from being fired on, and hit. One of the soldiers stepped forward – tall and stocky, with a scar running down the right side of his face. He held his left hand out.

Boucher pulled the boy in behind him.

"Not the hand-shaking type, are we?" the soldier said in a thick cockney accent as he withdrew his hand, placing it casually behind his back.

Boucher didn't reply.

"What's the matter? Are you a mute?"

"No."

"Good. Allow me the courtesy of an introduction then." He pointed to the man on his left. "This here is Sergeant Henry Bradford, and the men behind you are Privates Burnett and Wilson. And I'm Major Peter Hickman. Is this your boy?" He nodded at Rémy.

"That's none of your concern. Don't look at him."

"Woah," Hickman said, raising his hands out in front, as if to say, '*I come in peace*'. "No need for the hostility, friend. You will be safe here."

"Hostility? You guys open fired on us. And Matilda? Where did you drag her off to?"

The major looked to his sergeant.

"The woman needed urgent attention. Wilson will be looking after her down in Sick Bay in a few. And my apologies about the unpleasant welcome. We have to be careful."

Boucher grunted, still unsure of the situation.

"You don't look like one of the scientists?" Hickman said.

"Because I'm not one."

"How is it, then, that a man and boy randomly show up at a remote place like this? You can see my point of view on this, can't you, Mister? And by the looks of things, you need a doctor yourself, and that boy needs a warm meal in his belly."

Boucher didn't want to admit it but what choice did he have? His gut told him that something wasn't right here. *Soldiers don't run research stations.* But to refuse them meant going out into the dark with nothing.

"How is it that a bunch of British soldiers are running a research station?" he asked. "Look, we've come a long way—"

"I can see that."

He ran the situation through is head. Whatever was going on here, the reality was that they were starving, cold, and filthy, and out of options.

"Okay, Mister," Hickman said, "I'll tell you what. Just come in. Let us get a warm meal into that boy. There's plenty of hot water for you two to wash, and we can even offer you a private room with comfortable beds."

Boucher didn't reply. Exhaustion was trying to shut his body down but something about Hickman wasn't right. He struggled to shake away fatigue.

"Still not good enough?" Hickman asked.

"I don't think they have a choice, Sir," Burnett said, looking the boy up and down.

Hickman's eyes widened, his brows raising. "Come on, let the doc take a look at you. You wouldn't last a second out here after lights-out. Speaking of which, that happens in one hour. So, how about it, eh? Let's get you clean and fattened up. We'll talk in the morning."

Boucher released a held breath and nodded his acquiescence. What choice did he have? Keeping the boy close, he followed the soldiers into the station, catching a strange, unfamiliar smell as they walked down a corridor. Gas-powered lamps were placed every few yards on the walls. A silent light source – perfect for night.

"Here we are," Hickman announced, showing them a door. Inside, were two single beds, with fresh sheets.

Boucher felt like he owed the soldiers an apology and a thanks but he wasn't able to speak as he drifted towards the bed.

"Get some rest, gentlemen. I've sent one of the lads to fetch you both something to eat. There is a toilet facility with clean towels, etc." He nodded at the en suite. "Wilson will be in to take a look at those wounds shortly."

Boucher nodded a silent thanks.

"We run a tight ship here. Breakfast is at zero-seven-hundred. And don't worry, Burnett will look after your rifle. But, please... make yourselves at home."

After a while, Boucher couldn't hear any more words. He couldn't help but think they'd found an oasis in the middle of the artic. Old world comforts that he'd taken for granted, especially the biggest bonus of all coming from Private Wilson, who tended to their wounds. Getting undressed for examination was an effort for both of them – their bodies beaten and burned out. But a welcome rejuvenation came in the form of warm soup, painkillers, and some fresh clothes for the morning.

He'd never seen the boy so happy and, despite everything, he felt grateful for the hospitality. When their heads hit their respective pillow, that was it.

When the breakfast call came – a rap on

the door – he pushed himself up from the bed and found the boy sound asleep in the one next to him. They hadn't realized how exhausted they were until they'd laid their heads down. He sat up and went to the window to see a dull sky meet snowy hills and frozen fjord. Wild and beautiful, without a sound.

Below the window, one of the soldiers walked by as if conducting a perimeter check. He passed a large grey propane tank, with piping connected to the station.

The door to their room swung open and Private Burnett entered.

Boucher stepped forward, almost defensively, ready to attack if he got close to the boy.

"Relax, Mister," Burnett said. He was no more than nineteen or twenty, with a thick Yorkshire accent. "Just bringing you guys some fresh towels. Major said you need to wash up and then come join us in the mess for breakfast. Wilson will be in to dress those wounds again afterwards. How's the pain?"

"A bit better, I suppose..."

"Here," he said, holding out an open hand, "take these. They'll help."

Boucher examined his offerings – two white and blue capsules with *Ponstan* printed on them. "Cheers."

The billet was clean and appeared freshly painted, and that's when he realized he wasn't cold.

He looked over at the en suite door, feeling like he was in a student accommodation – easily the best place he'd been since St. Johns. The bathroom was larger than he expected, and the sight of a toilet made him laugh. He inspected the walk-in shower, turned it on, and took a moment to relish warm water against his hand. Bliss.

He removed the dressing around his waist and gagged at the blood and pus stains. Beneath it, fresh stitches sealed what had been his gaping wound. He couldn't help but feel they were tended to just in time.

A bit wobbly, he held onto the frame as he pulled himself into the shower, which felt like stepping into heaven.

Warm water ran all over his body, through his hair and beard and, for a few moments, he lost himself in the euphoria of it all. Rivulets of dirt struggled down the plughole.

An hour later, with their wounds re-patched, they looked at themselves in the mirror and couldn't recognise the two strangers staring back. The soldiers had provided a scissors, a razor, and other toiletries. Boucher couldn't help but smile at how smart the boy looked after a haircut and shower – a total transformation – and for the second time in as long as he could remember, the kid looked genuinely happy.

He supposed a price couldn't be put on dignity, but he worried about the boy settling in too quickly. Yes, they'd been looked after but still something didn't sit right with him. Why were the soldiers here? Did the woman get the same hospitality as they did? A multitude of concerns and questions swirled around his head.

"Dad, I'm hungry."

"Wanna get some breakfast?"

"Yes."

The smell of fried meat drew them to the mess hall, where a long table took up the centre, with an empty plate in front of the three soldiers present – evidence of a meal enjoyed.

Major Hickman stood in welcome and ushered them to vacant seats at the end of the table. One of the privates made a joke about how clean they were, but didn't get the response he'd hoped for.

"Breakfast was an hour ago," Hickman said, "but I'll allow an exception for you today. Burnett is a decent cook. He'll fix you something up."

Boucher didn't reply and could tell his manner was starting to annoy Hickman, who leaned in, making direct eye contact. "Still not saying much?"

"Where's Matilda?"

"She is fine. Tell me... What is her full name?"

"I don't know."

Hickman gave a derisive half-laugh as he leaned back in his chair. "It seems nobody has names anymore. Just a bunch of strangers wandering around the Arctic."

"Exactly," Boucher said.

"And what about you, boy?" He turned his attention to the youngster.

"R-Rémy..."

Boucher shot the boy a stern look that didn't go unnoticed by the soldiers.

"Now that wasn't so hard, was it? And your old man here? Does he have a name—"

"Stop talking to him. The name's Boucher. Look, Major, we need time to adjust. It has been a long journey for us to this point. And the truth is, our first encounter with your men wasn't exactly friendly. You took the woman away—"

"And we looked after you. Fed, watered, and fresh clothes. Not to mention, Wilson here stopped that wound from bleeding out. What more do you want? I told you, she is in Sick Bay. You can go see her after you eat something.

You and your boy are skin and bone. You need to get some meat onto you. And I don't appreciate your lack of trust in me, Mister Boucher." He let out a frustrated sigh, then clicked his fingers at Burnett, who brought over plates and set them in front of Boucher and the boy. "My job is to look after everyone here. After you eat, we'll take a walk and I'll address your concerns."

Boucher nodded, still unsure of the situation. On his plate sat a lump of fatty fried meat resembling pork. It looked heavily salted and was tough to cut.

"It's the best we can do," Sergeant Bradford remarked.

Boucher and the boy were starving and tucked into the meal. The overwhelming taste of overcooked and salted fat caught his breath and brought on a fit of coughing. Some of the soldiers laughed, but Hickman shouted them into silence.

He controlled his cough with a large mouthful of water and finished his meal.

Afterwards, Hickman escorted them

out into the hallway. "You're a pilot, aren't you?" he said as they sat on the staircase at the entrance to the station.

Boucher struggled to hide his surprise.

"I recognised the emblems on the boy's clothing yesterday. It's your overcoat, isn't it?"

Boucher kept quiet.

"Either that or you killed a pilot and took it... My guess is, you and the boy crashed a few miles from here, picked up the transmission, and came looking for some semblance of the life you had before all this madness happened."

Boucher let out a loud sigh, turning his gaze towards the frozen fjord. "Yes, you're right, that is my overcoat. While you seem to have me all figured out, I, however, can't understand why a bunch of British soldiers are up here in a research station, playing house. Where are Matilda and the others?"

"Boucher, I suspect our reasons for being here aren't too different. When those things came one night, we were given orders to return home and help maintain control. Which is funny, because control was the one thing we didn't have. An illusion. You can't control the uncontrollable."

"What are they?"

"We don't know... yet."

Boucher looked to him, waiting for an answer that never came.

"What we do know is that every major city across Europe now lies in ruins. They are nocturnal and anything caught in their swarm is devoured in a matter of seconds."

"Can I see the woman now?"

"Shortly..."

Boucher rubbed his temples against his growing anxiety.

"Why do you care so much for this woman? Is she your lover?"

Boucher looked at the boy, who sat quietly playing with one of his figurines. He couldn't be sure if he was listening or not. "He lost his mother... and is attached."

"I see." Hickman nodded. "If it's any

consolation, all my men lost wives and mothers, too. But the new world doesn't have time for our grief. The only thing that matters now is survival. And here in ZERO, I am in charge. And our survival is paramount."

Boucher studied his face, unable to tell if he was well-adjusted or a bit mad. His mind raced through a tangle of scenarios as fear and worry bubbled close to the surface. "Where are the others?"

"Who?" Hickman asked, his brows furrowed.

"The people who worked here. Scientists and—"

"They're all gone. Like everyone else in the world." His eyes narrowed and, for the first time, Boucher sensed he was getting uncomfortable.

"I suppose we now live in a time where only the fittest survive. Come on, Mister Pilot, let me show you to Sick Bay."

They were greeted at the door by Private Wilson, who blocked them from entering.

Hickman demanded an explanation, and was told that the woman had taken a bad turn and he needed to perform a procedure on her.

Boucher grabbed the boy's hand, pulled him close, and eyeballed the private. "I want to see her."

"I'm sorry, Major," Wilson said, ignoring Boucher, "I can't let anyone in. I need a couple of hours without, err... interruptions."

A loud scream came from inside. "We've run out of painkillers and I don't know if I can contain the infection."

"Stop ignoring me and let me in," Boucher demanded.

"Sorry, Mister. I can't do that."

"Move!"

"Wilson is a great medic," Hickman said. "He fixed you—"

"What is going on here?" Boucher demanded. "What the hell is going on?" The boy tugged at him, no doubt scared at the escalating situation. Boucher couldn't contain his anger any longer and, without warning, pushed past the two soldiers and kicked the door open with his toeless foot, his momentum sending him tumbling forward to the floor.

When he looked up, he expected to see a doctor's surgery-type room, with a clean bed and maybe some overhead lights, with the woman laid up resting. But, to his horror, the room before him resembled a butcher's shop.

"Dad?" the boy called.

He scrambled to his feet, taking in the white walls with chipped paint and blood splatter in every corner. In the centre, a bed without a mattress and a screaming mess of a person.

"Matilda!" he cried.

Above her, hanging from what looked like meat hooks, her severed arms dangled like marinating cold cuts. A rank stench of her excrement hit him hard but he couldn't look away from the screaming woman on the bed, armless, with both legs filleted down to the bone.

"Dad!" the boy called again.

He turned to face him, and the last thing he saw was the butt-end of a rifle flash in front of his face.

Boucher woke to the boy calling his name. Through his blurred vision, he could barely make out his face – the sound of his voice reminding him of being underwater. Everything inside his head spun and the right side of his face felt too tight. A few seconds later, his vision cleared, then his nostrils filled with an odour that made him want to retch, but his limp body didn't connect.

"Dad, please wake up," the boy begged.

"I'm here," he muttered, his voice croaky and raw. He sat up, taking in his surroundings, finding himself in the middle of a strange room, with padded walls, ceiling, and floor, all moist and filthy. No windows other than a small square slot that sat three-quarters of the way up the door. It reminded him of something from an old institution, only the padding seemed to be nailed, which displayed a serious lack of professional craftsmanship.

"Are you okay?" he asked the boy.

"Yes. After they hit you, they put us in here."

"How long was I out?"

"About an hour," a man said from the other side of the room.

Boucher turned to see a figure crouched in the corner, cloaked in shadow – featureless.

"His name is Jürgen," the boy said.

For a moment, Boucher thought he was hallucinating, but several blinks and a slow shake of the head told him he wasn't. "Jürgen?"

"Yes," the boy answered.

He got to his feet and checked the boy for physical marks. "Are you sure you're okay?"

"The boy is fine," Jürgen said, his accent Germanic. "He is a very bright boy. We were talking while you rested—"

"Shut up. What the fuck is going on here?"

"Well, it seems to me," Jürgen began, "you both have been placed on the menu, too."

"What are you talking about?"

"Well, our British friends out there... In their survival efforts, it seems that they acquired a taste for... their fellow man." He struggled to his feet and stepped out of the shadows. And that's when Boucher noticed he was missing an arm.

"What happened? What is this place?"

Jürgen smirked, as if at peace with his predicament. "Well, you're alive. So, you must know all about the rest of the world by now?"

"Yes..."

"I'm a scientist. My team and I live here. We study the atmosphere, melting ice, you know, things like that. However, when the creatures... How do you say... dismantled?"

"Destroy?" he offered.

"Yes, destroy. When they destroyed everything... Well, society collapsed. My team were up here in the Arctic in relative safety. Well, as long as we kept quiet at night. We established a rescue broadcast in the hope that people who fled the cities might find us and we could help..."

"How many of you are left?" Boucher asked.

"I believe I am the last person. Our transmission was picked up by Hickman and his mercenaries. I believe they went a wall."

"A wall?"

"How do you say?"

"AWOL?"

"Right. Yes. Going rogue, or something to that effect. Anyway, they came here—"

A bang against the door cut him off, followed by one of the soldiers ordering them to stop talking.

He continued in a whisper, telling them how Hickman took over the complex, prioritizing the rations for his men. "We are just scientists. What could we do against armed psychopaths? They consumed everything – all our food – and took the best quarters. Before we knew it, we were their prisoners."

"Why didn't you leave?" the boy asked.

Jürgen smiled. "My dear boy, not all of us have a survival expert like your father guiding us, eh? The Arctic is no place for wandering without experience or supplies."

"I'm no survival expert. I'm just trying to get my boy to safety."

"Ha, well, I'm sorry to tell you, my friend... whatever safety you were searching for, isn't here. You only found hell."

Boucher looked the German up and down, trying to decide if the story was the truth or the ramblings of a madman. "This padded room?"

"Ha, homemade soundproofing." He shook his head. "Good for keeping the livestock silent, eh?"

"What d'you mean?"

"Haven't you figured it out yet?" He turned to reveal the butchery wound where his arm used to be. "We are keeping them alive—"

With a loud crash, the door swung open. Boucher and boy were cast aside by the soldiers barging in.

The German attempted to put up a fight with one arm but was soon overpowered, knocked to the floor, and dragged out by his feet. "Kill yourselves!" he screamed back to Boucher. "Don't wait any longer, kill yourself and the boy. They will eat you both! Kill yourselves!"

As his words disappeared with him out of view, Hickman entered the room and stood towering over them. "I see you met Jürgen. Nice chap when you get to know him." He laughed. "I'm sure the lads and I will enjoy our German steak dinner tonight."

Boucher recoiled in horror, shielding the boy as best he could.

Hickman dropped down on his hunkers and glared at them. "Don't worry. We won't eat the only man who can fly a plane around here. We may have use for your skillset..."

For a moment, Boucher felt some relief.

"The same can't be said for the boy. Burnett has his eye on him." Hickman smirked, rising up and making his way to the door. "You need to think about that when it comes to what you have to offer."

"You're a fucking monster!" Boucher called after him.

"That's where you're wrong," Hickman stated. "Times have changed, Mister Boucher. We must adapt in order to overcome. Otherwise this world belongs to the reavers."

It was as long a night as he could remember. And he held the boy close as they huddled in the corner, dreading the door opening again. When it did, three of Hickman's men entered, dragged him out, and left the boy locked inside.

He didn't resist. What was the point? The situation had become hopeless. They took him to the far end of the research station, where Hickman had an office. He sat behind the desk with his feet up, staring at Boucher as he was plonked onto a chair facing him. The privates left the room.

"I hope you slept well?"

Boucher didn't reply, looking towards the window, the daylight barely noticeable.

"I'll get straight to it, Mister Boucher. We have a plane. But, unfortunately, we don't have anyone who can fly it. Arctic winters last a long time, with little or no daylight, and food is becoming scarce. My thinking is, you take the plane out for an hour each morning and help Bradford survey the area for food."

"And if I refuse?"

"Well, then, I'm afraid you won't see your boy."

That thought made him want to kill the man but he knew he'd be dead before he got to him. The soldiers outside were no doubt listening. "So, we are prisoners here now?"

Hickman got to his feet and walked to the window. Boucher didn't need to look to know that the fjord formed his immediate view. "Try see it from my perspective. I have three men, four including myself, who need food, shelter, and some shred of hope that what we are doing here is for something."

"Murder and cannibalism—"

"Survival!" he snapped, turning to face him. He closed the distance between them, so close, Boucher caught his putrid breath. "Survival, Mister Boucher." He stepped back. "I'm not proud of the things we've done here but I am proud of our ability to adapt to this new world. We are alive. The night is a hunting ground for those creatures and no weapon can contain them once they hone in on something they can eat."

"So, why fight it?" Boucher barked. "Why not just give up?"

"Last week, I found Burnett in his room with a gun in his mouth. He said the same thing. *'What's the point anymore? The world has ended.'* He cleared his throat. "That statement almost insults me. What was I supposed to do? Give up? Not do my best for my men? They need a leader, and a leader can't lead without giving them something to live for."

"And you think torturing me and my boy is giving them something to live for?"

141

"No. You're a means to an end. I told my men that we'd have to do whatever we could to survive the winter here, and if we get out the other side, we can leave this place and fly south."

Boucher laughed, rubbing his temples to fight back the tension threatening to crack open his skull. "You're a mad man!"

Hickman snorted. "Am I?" His mouth turned up in a sneer. "I'm maintaining morale, and my plan is good. We wait out the winter here, those things will die of starvation, and then we can take our planet back."

"Do you honestly believe that?"

Hickman looked at him with a glint of madness in his eyes and nodded. "I have to... Come with me, let me show you something."

Boucher was convinced the major and his men were walking him into certain death. They made their way down the main gravel track, its surface covered in salt, glistening with licks of frost. He had a vision of being dragged around the back of a building and executed, his carcass used to feed the troops, the horror continuing until they turned on the boy. With nowhere to run to, all he could do was shake it from his head, draw in a deep cold breathe, and release it at a slow, steady pace.

To his surprise, Hickman had been telling the truth – there was a plane. A Basler BT-67, just like his, only this silver bird was in pristine condition. He turned to find Hickman staring at him.

"Well, Mister Boucher, can you pilot that machine?"

"Yes."

"Good." He nodded to his men. "Bring him back to the holding cell."

Boucher paced around the cell, his stomach churning, heart racing. There had to be a way out, and the plane seemed to be their only chance. But it could only happen with the boy included.

Rémy, sitting on the floor, mumbled something Boucher didn't catch. He

143

stopped pacing when the smell hit him and he realized what had happened. The boy was whimpering, red-faced. Guilt slammed into him and he knelt beside the kid, assuring him that everything was okay.

"I'm going to get us out of here, Rémy." He removed his jacket and shirt, using the latter to clean the boy.

"Tonight, when they bring us food, I need you to do something—"

"Why didn't you tell Jürgen about Matilda?"

"How could I, son? His one comfort was the thought of her escaping this place. He deserved to take that with him."

"He deserved nothing!"

"Don't say that, Rémy. What's the matter with you?"

"It was because of him the reavers are here. I hate him! I hate him for taking Mom." He burst into tears.

Boucher rubbed his son's cheeks with his thumbs. "You're right. You hear me? You're right."

The boy looked up with watery eyes.

"I need you to keep it together. We can't lose hope now. We need to work together, son. Can you do that for me?"

The boy nodded as he whispered a plan into his ear. Despite the fear gripping him inside, he had to act, knowing this would be their last chance to escape this hell. Yes, the reavers had ruined everything they'd ever known, but what they'd found in ZERO plunged them into the darkest side of humanity. Trusting in the shred of hope they possessed might offer them their only chance of survival.

The day crawled by, making the wait for the soldiers to come with their rations feel so much longer. At the sound of footsteps on the other side of the door, Boucher signalled for the boy to begin.

He dropped to the floor in a fit of coughing and convulsing, thrashed around while Boucher hammered his fist against the door. "Help me! Hurry. Get in here and help my boy."

The hatch opened and an eye

appeared, flicking left and right, then down at the convulsing boy, now foaming at the mouth. When Burnett entered, he made a beeline for the boy, then shouted back to the other men to go get the medic. "This has to be some sort of seizure." He looked to Boucher for an answer.

"He has epilepsy," Boucher said, then checked to see if the corridor was clear. When Burnett roll the boy onto his side, he lunged forward and grabbed for the pistol holstered at his waist.

Burnett jerked, grasping hold of Boucher's wrist, the pistol springing free and clattering to the floor.

"You stupid bastard," he shouted, pulling Boucher into him, his forehead cracking hard against the bridge of his nose.

Boucher dropped to the floor, holding his face, tears and blood blurring his vision. Then he was lifted by a kick to his ribs, but he didn't have time to register the pain as he was hammered with a flurry of punches and boots to his head and torso. He curled up, only to be stamped on the head, his skull slamming off the concrete floor. In desperation, he flailed out with his hands to find anything to aid his plight – to no avail, the hits kept coming in.

The boy screamed, begging Burnett to stop kicking his father to death, but his words fell on deaf ears.

"When I'm done with you, Boucher, I'm gonna spit-roast your body and fuck that boy into oblivion." He continued kicking and stomping, until a sharp crack reverberated through the space, followed by a deafening silence.

Gasping for breath, Boucher looked up to see Burnett back away from him and slump against the padded wall – his confused gaze snapping left and right as blood trickled from his mouth.

On the other side of the room, the boy held the pistol, his hand trembling – the act beyond his comprehension.

"It's okay," Boucher said, moving over to him. "It's alright, Rémy."

The boy didn't reply, his gaze fixed on the dying soldier, watching him exit the world with slow gasps.

"Dad?"

"It's okay. Give me the gun."

"But—"

"You did what you had to do, son," he whispered, easing the pistol from the boy's grip, his eyes full of terror. "You did what needed to be done, son. I'm proud of you. But we don't have time to linger on this, you hear me?"

The boy nodded, pulling his focus from the dead soldier.

"The others will have heard the shot. We have to get moving."

Snow and ice crunched underfoot as they hurried away from the research station, where the soldiers could be heard shouting and arguing among themselves. Boucher figured Hickman hadn't planned on dinner escaping, and he was thankful for that. It bought them time.

The near-dark conditions would offer a cloak, or at least that's what he hoped. They ran down the main path, opting to go around the back of the small green building at the end of the row. Using his elbow, he shattered a small pane of glass beside the back door and took the boy inside, where they huddled by a window overlooking the main path. At the far end, the remaining soldiers could be seen preparing to search. Boucher knew they'd be checking every inch of the research complex but, for the first time, he was thankful for pitch-darkness descending around them all.

He struggled to contain his cough. His wounds had burst from Burnett's assault but he assured the boy that he was okay and only needed a little while to recoup his strength.

"They will do silent patrols now it's dark. And they know we'll be trying to get to the plane."

"But, Dad, we can't fly at night? Those things will—"

"We're not going for the plane..."

The boy didn't reply, confusion etched across his face.

Boucher patted his shoulder. "When

they embark on their mission, we will begin ours."

As night fell, silence accompanied the moonlight, its glow lighting the gravel path. Boucher watched the research station, with Hickman standing outside, giving his men instructions by hand signal. His message was clear. Armed with machetes and knives, the soldiers began walking down the main path as a light snow fluttered about.

"They're coming for us."

"What will we do?" the boy asked, his voice shaking.

"Listen, son." He pressed on his nose until a shot of pain subsided, then touched the boy's shoulder. "Those men will kill us on sight. They won't take any chance of us making noise. With them checking every building and the plane, we have to head back and hide."

"Okay."

At the back of the building, he spotted a small wooden shed, probably used to house tools. As good a hiding place as any.

They crouched inside, careful not to make a sound, listening to the soldiers' approach as they checked each premises. When they got to the green building at the end of the path, Boucher had the pistol ready.

"You can't shoot them," the boy whispered.

"Last resort."

With great relief, he didn't need to fire off a round, as the soldiers passed by without noticing them. As soon as the path was clear, they stepped out and snuck along the back of buildings until they came to the main research station.

The boy stayed by the main door to keep watch while Boucher went inside. Fear was a major factor now – if any loud noise was made, the reavers would be on them in seconds.

He wasted no time, emerging from the station with his rifle and a gas-powered lamp. The boy was told to hold firm at the corner, separated from him but also hidden from the searchers, while he made his way around to the propane tank.

Just as he finished releasing the valve on the tank, someone whistled, and he turned to see the boy racing over to him. He left the lamp in place, took the boy under his arm, and they hurried towards the fjord.

They found a spot and hunkered in the snow, waiting, the unbearable cold causing Boucher's hands to shake as he struggled to keep the rifle steady as he aimed at the propane tank.

"Look," the boy whispered, pointing at the returning soldiers.

"Are you ready, son?"

As soon as the main door closed with the soldiers inside, Boucher got to work, fighting to control his shaking hands. In his mind, he knew he'd only get one shot. He rubbed his eyes to clear any blurriness, then honed in on the lamp, steadied his breathing, applied first pressure, exhaled, then squeezed the trigger.

The explosion was louder than

expected, forcing the boy to recoil as a mix of orange and red erupted into the night sky. Men screamed and shouted inside the shattered building as they rushed to escape the blaze.

In their panic and confusion, Wilson and Bradford exited and opened fire into the darkness. Wild and aimless.

"Keep down!" Boucher said. Out in the cold darkness, a droning began. He grabbed the boy. "We have to move. They're coming, and we need to get inside."

A swarm of reavers descended on the burning station with a ferociousness that even took Boucher by surprise. The soldiers opened fired in a futile attempt to fend them off, but with every gunshot, the droning intensified, like a wasp's hive under attack. In a matter of seconds, the creatures were feasting on flesh as agonising screams echoed into the night. The boy watched in horror, his first proper look at the large black locust-like creatures.

Boucher took him by the arm and they moved fast and undetected around the burning station, the flames lighting their way down the main path. Clear of the building, they quickened their pace, the human screams now silenced – the burning remnants of humanity along with it, succumbed to the droning.

With the plane in sight, Boucher shouted encouragement to the boy, then, without warning, he hit the cold gravel track face-first, his mouth filling with dirt and salt.

The boy tried to help him up, but Boucher clutched his back, grimacing in agony. He hadn't heard the shot but looked to see Hickman standing at the top of the street, rifle in hand, lowering the scarf around his face to reveal a maniacal smile.

"Dad!" the boy screamed. "Please get up. Please!"

Boucher struggled to his knees, his heart throbbing as blood poured from his lower back. He pulled the boy around him, shielding him from Hickman, who walked towards them.

"Get to the plane," he said, his vision fading. "Hurry!"

"What about you?"

"I'm oka—"

Blood splattered across the boy's face and Boucher fell against him, knocking him on his back.

Shocked and terrified, Rémy stared at Hickman, who approached, ready to fire again.

Blood dripped from his father's mouth, his eyes rolling as he gagged and coughed. He pulled Rémy into him. "Run."

"Where?"

"The p-plane. Go... now."

"What about you?"

Hickman's footsteps drew closer.

"Rémy, listen to... me. Run. Now!" His father pushed himself up from the ground.

Shaking, Rémy inched back, watching his father turn and tackle Hickman, roaring at the top of his lungs. The two grappled, with the falling rifle letting off a loud shot that had him ducking. The sound was followed by an intense droning and, before a winner could be determined, a black swarm engulfed them both.

Rémy wanted to scream but his father's constant advice echoed in his head: that noise attracts the reavers. He couldn't decipher anything through the feeding frenzy, other than Hickman's deranged laugh.

With no other choice, he sprinted for the plane.

He hid in the cargo hold for the night, shaking, unable to sleep. Visions of his father haunted his thoughts. When morning broke, or what passed for a new day, he crept out and returned to the spot to find his remains, scattered over the gravel track – frozen. He sat there for a long time, weeping and groaning, then got up and walked around the complex. The reavers had gotten them all. With nothing left, he walked back and knelt beside what remained of his father, unable to hold back his sobs.

Two days later, having only moved from the spot to shelter in the plane at night, he decided to bury what was left. He carried the bundle to the bank of the fjord, praying in silence, wishing for him to be reunited with his mother. His father's words repeated over and over in his head as he laid him to rest: *How a man conducts himself at a funeral says a lot about his character.* He tried his best do it right but, inside, he felt empty and alone.

Later, he went back to the plane. Nowhere in his memory could he recall how to get it started. Whatever he did, nothing worked. The radio struggled to find anything beyond the wall of static. Maybe one day it would – he'd try it every day, just like his father had done with the beacon on the hill. For now, he would use the skills his father had taught him – feeding from boreholes in the fjord while keeping warm and silent at night. It was

the best he could do in this droning world
of nothingness.

THE END

"Outside, black ribbons of rain fall like an answer."

— 40 Watt Sun

ACKNOWLEGEMENTS

I honestly don't know where to start when it comes to this section of the book, simply because I have very little memory of writing it and am not exactly sure what to say about it. From somewhere in my hazy memory, I know I vomited out the first draft during the height of the pandemic back in 2020. That's not to say that this is a pandemic-inspired story... no, not at all. In fact, the seed for this story took root a few years prior and ever since the birth of my son, Samuel, I wanted to write something that explores a father and son relationship. Perhaps without knowing, the pandemic gave me the space and time to do that, even if it was not planned. So, I guess, I can't say the pandemic was all doom and gloom for me.

Anyway... if it wasn't for my crew of talented people who congregate beneath the Idolum umbrella, this book would not be in your hand right now. To my editor, Eamon Ó Cléirigh, my eternal gratitude will always be with you for your time and effort. Thank you. Without these gifts, this story would still be a vomited up first draft lying in a folder somewhere unfit for human consumption.

Interior design and artwork, my long-term collaborators, Kenneth W. Cain and Boz Mugabe once again delivered the goods.

In no particular order, the following friends, colleagues, reviewers and all-round good people make my little living space on this planet a bit more worthwhile; Nuzo Onoh, Gemma Amor, John Langan, Tim Waggoner, Michael Griffin, Alex J. Knudsen, Sadie Hartmann, John Mulvaney, Ben Eads, Janelle Janson, Ross Jeffrey, Paul Carroll,

Priya Sharma, T.E. Grau, Barry Keegan, Barry Maher, Gary Fox, Steve Stred, Anthony Duff, Derek Brady, Trevor Kennedy, Ray Palen, Adrian Coombe, Jude Purcell, Kevin McHugh, Jeremy Wagner, Sie Carroll and to those who have mentored me through the ups and downs of this writing game so far; Philip Fracassi, Adam Nevill, Joe Hill and Tim Lebbon – you guys continue to inspire and guide me. Always appreciated. Never forgotten.

To my darling wife, Orla, I just want to say I love you and our boys. Without our family, life has no purpose.

Finally, to the reader of this book... thank you for taking a punt on me. I hope you've been entertained and if so, will come visit again. Until next time...

ABOUT THE AUTHOR

SEÁN O'CONNOR is an award-nominated author, primarily known for his Horror and Speculative Fiction. He lives in Dublin, Ireland, with his wife and kids.

WEEPING SEASON

SEÁN O'CONNOR

In the spirit of Charlie Brooker's *Black Mirror* and *The Twilight Zone* comes Weeping Season — an unsettling, suspenseful chiller that leaves you gasping for breath...

A group of strangers wake up in a cold isolated forest with no memory of anything before their arrival. Lost, hungry and wandering aimlessly, they are summoned to a campsite by a remote entity who controls their fate through a series of tortuous objectives. Their only hope for survival is either escape from the psychological game reserve, known as Block 18, or face mortality at the hands of its maniacal moderator, who loves nothing more than watch his participants suffer...

"Fast, thrilling, and brutal, Weeping Season leaves you gasping for breath. O'Connor's prose is sharp and lean, and he has a great eye for the grisly. Thoroughly recommended."
— **Tim Lebbon**

ALSO AVAILABLE FROM
IDOLUM

KEENING COUNTRY

SEÁN O'CONNOR

A collection of experimental fiction ranging from creepy horror to powerful explorations of the human mind... ...In *Aerials*, strange antennas dot the landscape from out of nowhere and a tech worker's sister has been found dead, trusting her into a race against time to discover the truth before lies become fact... ...*Down Below* is a story about a boy who stumbles upon a dark family secret beneath the garden shed. A secret his father would do anything to keep buried... ...*Seven Years Gone* is a creepy tale of loss and suffering in which a train driver struggles to overcome haunting visions of his dearly departed... ...In *The Obsessed*, a young girl is infatuated with the older man next door. However, her dream crush has a lust that she will never be able to quench — unless she acquires a similar appetite...

"Visceral, compelling, *Keening Country* packs a considerable punch.
Read it and keep your eyes peeled for O'Connor's next work."
— **John Langan**
Author of *Children of the Fang and Other Genealogies*

ALSO AVAILABLE FROM

IDOLUM

THE BLACKENING

SEÁN O'CONNOR

When a young woman goes missing near the
sleepy Icelandic village of Vík, police inspector
John Ward wants to cancel the Northern Lights
Festival after his sole witness describes the
kidnapper as a "*Shadow*". However, police
commissioner Kári Ingason overrules him, fearing
the loss of tourist revenue will cripple the village.
Scientist Rakel Atladóttir and her peculiar
assistant Rúnar offer to help Ward investigate the
disappearance, plunging the trio into a fight for
survival, with the fate of humanity in jeopardy
against a malevolent cosmic horror...

"A feast of good old-fashioned horror, with
conflicted characters,

a gooey monster, and plenty of blood and guts."
— **Tim Waggoner**

Author of *The Forever House* & Bram Stoker
Award Winner